Abigail knew her cheeks were bright red.

"Thank you for being so nice about this, Ethan. The gossip must be embarrassing for you."

Ethan knitted his brows. "Are you kidding? These ladies just made my day. Apparently, I'm the most eligible Amish bachelor in Kent County."

He leaned forward. "And speaking of such things, a pretty, smart woman like yourself— it will only be a matter of time before someone asks to court you." He held her gaze. "Almost makes me think I ought to—" He cut himself off.

Abigail hesitated. He'd been about to say something, but what? She thought to press him, but then her mother took off and she had to hurry after her. "See you tomorrow," she said.

"Tomorrow," Ethan answered. "Hey, Abby. What kind of cake are you making?"

"Lemon icebox," she responded. She didn't look back, but she could feel him watching her. Had he been about to ask if he could court her? Abigail's heart gave a little pitter-patter…

Emma Miller lives quietly in her old farmhouse in rural Delaware. Fortunate enough to have been born into a family of strong faith, she grew up on a dairy farm, surrounded by loving parents, siblings, grandparents, aunts, uncles and cousins. Emma was educated in local schools and once taught in an Amish schoolhouse. When she's not caring for her large family, reading and writing are her favorite pastimes.

Books by Emma Miller

Love Inspired

The Amish Spinster's Courtship
The Christmas Courtship
A Summer Amish Courtship

The Amish Matchmaker

A Match for Addy
A Husband for Mari
A Beau for Katie
A Love for Leah
A Groom for Ruby
A Man for Honor

Hannah's Daughters

Courting Ruth
Miriam's Heart
Anna's Gift

Visit the Author Profile page at Harlequin.com for more titles.

A Summer Amish Courtship

Emma Miller

2020

Happy Mother's Day

To Mom

Love Steven

LOVE INSPIRED

INSPIRATIONAL ROMANCE

LOVE INSPIRED®

INSPIRATIONAL ROMANCE

Recycling programs
for this product may
not exist in your area.

ISBN-13: 978-1-335-48811-4

A Summer Amish Courtship

Copyright © 2020 by Emma Miller

This edition published by arrangement with Harlequin Books S.A.

For questions and comments about the quality of this book,
please contact us at CustomerService@Harlequin.com.

Love Inspired
22 Adelaide St. West, 40th Floor
Toronto, Ontario M5H 4E3, Canada
www.Harlequin.com

Printed in U.S.A.

Two are better than one.
—Ecclesiastes 4:9

Chapter One

"Tietscher!" eight-year-old Mary Fisher cried. She ran up the steps, her prayer *kapp* strings bouncing, and through the open doorway into the cloakroom of the schoolhouse. In the cold months, coats, cloaks and hats were hung on hooks on the wall. In the warmer months, it became a clutter catchall for lunch pails, fishing poles, overlooked homework and muddy boots. "Teacher, come quick!"

Ethan Miller was busy lining up his students' lunch boxes on two shelves he'd built and just hung on the back wall. Without the shelves, the lunch boxes, bags and pails were all over the floor and constantly being knocked over. That morning, a peanut butter and raisin bread sandwich wrapped in wax paper had ended up on the bottom of someone's shoe and John B. had enjoyed Ethan's egg salad for lunch. Ethan had had an apple.

"Tietscher!" Mary exclaimed, waving both hands in the air. "It's him again!"

"English, please," Ethan instructed. He slid a wrinkled brown paper sack with the name Jacob S. scrawled across it onto the lower shelf. He'd painted the shelving a dark navy blue and he had to admit, for having made it from pine scraps from his father's woodpile, it had turned out nicely. "What's going on?"

The petite third grader huffed, peering at him through tiny wire-framed eyeglasses. She switched to English. "He's going to knock it over and she's inside!"

Ethan liked Mary Fisher. She was a good student and was kind to the younger children, but she could also be a tattletale. Which was probably expected from a girl who was the youngest of a family of fifteen children. The Fishers ran the youth group in Hickory Grove and everyone joked that it made sense considering the fact that they had enough children to have a youth group of their own.

Ethan looked down at Mary, trying not to be perturbed by the interruption. Not only did Mary Fisher like to tattle, but she tended to add drama to any event. A scratch on an arm became a broken bone. A boy tossing a stone could become a gang of teens throwing rocks and sticks.

Ethan took a moment to calm his irritation. His students had been outside only ten minutes without his supervision. All he wanted to do was finish installing the shelves. How much trouble could anyone get into in ten minutes? And he'd left two fifteen-year-old girls in charge, girls who could certainly be counted on to keep an eye on younger children for a few minutes.

Apparently they *couldn't* be trusted today.

Ethan didn't usually have recess this late in the day. In an hour he would dismiss his students, but it was so pretty outside, and spring had been late in coming that year. The students were all eager to get out into the sunshine after such a long, cold winter. That was why he'd given them half an hour, time enough for him to hang the new shelves. His plan was to then bring his students in and have a spelling bee. It was one of the events he had planned for their end-of-the-year program, which was to include a fund-raiser, the exact nature of which had yet to be decided.

Ethan added a tin lunch bucket to one of the shelves. "Who are we talking about, Mary?"

"Jamie Stolz!"

Ethan exhaled impatiently. He should have known.

Jamie was his new student. He'd been with them only six weeks. And in those six weeks the boy had caused more turmoil than the other twenty-six students put together in his one-room schoolhouse. Ethan squinted. "*What's* he going to do?"

"That's what I'm trying to tell you. He's rocking the girls' outhouse," Mary wailed, pushing her glasses up the bridge of her nose. "He's going to knock it over and Elsie Yoder is inside!"

"What?" Ethan looked down at the little girl, certain he'd misheard.

Mary's head bobbed, hands flapping. "Jamie is rocking the outhouse and he says he's going to knock it over! With Elsie inside!"

Ethan strode past his student. "Jamie Stolz!" he bellowed taking the schoolhouse steps two at a time. Behind the one-room building, he spotted a group of children gathered around the two outhouses that stood side by side, one for boys, one for girls. Both had small privacy fences in front of them.

"What's going on here?" Ethan asked, walking across the grass. Off to the left he saw several boys involved in a game of softball. To the far right, a group of teen girls huddled in a tight circle, their heads together, oblivious to the outhouse drama. His two appointed guardians were among them.

"Jamie, Teacher," Alfie, a third grader answered morosely. He hooked his thumbs through his suspenders. "He's being bad again."

Just then, a squeal arose from behind the girls' privacy fence. "Help!"

Ethan could see the top of the outhouse above the fence. It didn't appear to be rocking. But then he'd dug the foundations for the new outhouses the previous summer so he knew they were pretty stable.

"Elsie?" Ethan called.

"Teacher!" she shrieked.

Ethan halted at the little fence and peered under it. He didn't see Jamie.

Ethan hesitated, not sure what to do. It wouldn't be proper of him to go to the outhouse door with the little girl inside. "Elsie, just come out here!"

"I can't get out!" Elsie shrieked. "Door's stuck!"

"Jamie? Where are you?" Ethan called sternly. Then he heard a loud rapping on the rear wall of the outhouse.

Elsie began to cry.

"Mary Judith!" Ethan called in the direction of the cluster of teen girls who were still unaware of what was going on. "Could you come get your sister?"

The blonde teen with a blue scarf tied on her head looked up in surprise to hear her name and then hurried toward him.

"Go see if you can get your sister out," Ethan instructed. He turned around to the other students gathered in a semicircle. They were all talking at once. One of his first graders was crying. "Recess is over," he declared, pointing toward the schoolhouse. "Inside. Peter, get the boys off the ball field," he told one of his more responsible students.

Then, as Mary Judith walked behind the privacy fence, Ethan headed for the rear of the outhouses, which were on the edge of a small copse of trees. The woods were just beginning to spring to life and everywhere were shoots of new green leaves. "Jamie!" he called. "Jamie Stolz!"

Ethan came around the corner to see blond-haired Jamie shoving a thick branch between the girls' outhouse and its foundation. "Jamie," he barked just as the boy prepared to leap on the branch. And rock the outhouse again.

"Yes?" the little boy asked, taking a stumbling step back.

"I have her, Teacher," Mary Judith called from the other side of the outhouse. "Someone put a stick through the latch!"

"Everyone inside!" Ethan ordered again to the stragglers who'd not heard or obeyed his first command, trying not to transfer his displeasure with Jamie to the other children. He imagined they were as frustrated with the boy as he was. He was a constant disruption in the classroom: talking, throwing bits of paper, rocking loudly in his chair. And on the playground, he spent most of his time teasing younger children. "Everyone in the schoolhouse. Now, please." He turned back to his errant student. "Jamie, why would you do this?"

The boy tucked his hands behind his back. He was wearing denim pants, a pale blue shirt, suspenders and a straw hat. He looked like the other male students, yet he didn't. Most boys in Hickory Grove wore hand-me-downs. The clothes Jamie wore, though homemade like everyone else's, were all brand-spanking-new.

Ethan grabbed the stick Jamie had shoved under the outhouse and tossed it into the woods. "How did Elsie get locked inside?"

"I don't know."

Ethan pressed his lips together and glanced away, trying to calm the anger rising from his chest. If there was one thing he couldn't abide, it was a liar. He returned his gaze to his new student. "Did you lock Elsie in the outhouse?"

The boy stared at the ground.

"Why were you trying to tip it over?" Ethan pressed. "Jamie, if the outhouse had tipped over with her inside, Elsie could have been seriously hurt."

Jamie kicked at a pile of acorns on the ground. "I wasn't going to knock it over. Too heavy. I was just rocking it."

Ethan exhaled, looking away again. He was momentarily unsure what to do. He'd certainly encountered mischief since he'd accepted the job of the Hickory Grove schoolmaster two years ago, but it always had been the same sort of innocent naughtiness: frogs in lunch pails, the snapping of suspenders, the tugging of *kapp* strings. Until Jamie's arrival, the biggest problem he'd had was little boys arriving at school late because they stopped along the way to throw rocks in a pond.

Ethan looked at Jamie. "Have you something to say for yourself?" He opened his arms wide. "Anything?"

The boy concentrated on his new leather boots that looked as if they'd never been in a barn.

Ethan thought for a moment. He'd already talked with Jamie's widowed mother three times in the last six weeks. Three times! That was more than he'd spoken to other parents *since September*.

Abigail Stolz seemed like a nice enough woman. Though each time he approached her she was defensive, suggesting it was he who was responsible for her son's misbehavior. As if a schoolmaster was solely in charge of his students' discipline. And she was forward for an Amish woman, which had annoyed him the first time he met her, then amused him the second time. Truth was, she reminded him a lot of his stepsister Lovey, a woman who wasn't shy about speaking her mind. And he adored Lovey.

Ethan glanced down at Jamie. He didn't see any way out of this. He knew what he needed to do. "Get in my buggy," he ordered. With the warmer weather, he'd started walking to school again. It was less than a mile's walk if he cut across the fields, less than two if he took the road home. He'd only brought the buggy this morning because he'd intended to run into Byler's store after school and order a piece of stovepipe. He and his father were installing a woodstove to keep their shop warm where they were making a buggy.

Jamie looked up at Ethan. *"What?"*

"I said get in my buggy. I'll send one of the big boys out to hitch up Butter." Butter was his horse. Her name was Butterscotch. His dead wife had named her that after they bought the dun at an auction. She had said the mare was the color of her homemade butterscotch pudding. His Mary had teased him that the mare wasn't the proper color for an Amish man's buggy, but Ethan had bought her anyway. Because his Mary had liked her. He'd been razzed for years about the color of his driving horse and her name. He didn't care. She was one of the few things he had left of his wife.

"I don't understand," Jamie said. His English was excellent. Often children started school with no knowledge of the English language. In Kent County, Delaware, children usually strictly spoke Pennsylvania *Deitsch*—a form of German, not Dutch, as many Englishers mistakenly thought they used—in their homes, so it was up to the schoolmaster to teach them English. Ethan had been concerned when Jamie had arrived from out of state that he would have come from a school where the children were taught in Pennsylvania *Deitsch*. It happened in some places. But his concerns had been quickly dispelled; Jamie spoke English as well as Ethan did. And his diction might have been better.

"What do you not understand?" Ethan asked, beginning to lose his patience again. He was exasperated that the boy wasn't better behaved and exasperated with himself that he wasn't able to get him to act better. He was also annoyed with the child's mother. It was evident that she wasn't disciplining him. "I want you to get in my buggy and wait for me. I'm dismissing everyone early. And I'm taking you home." He pointed at the boy. "So I can speak to your mother. *Again.*"

Jamie met Ethan's gaze and he thrust out his lower lip. "You're being mean to me. Everyone here is mean to me. I don't like this school."

"Jamie, no one is—" Ethan halted midsentence. There was no sense arguing with a nine-year-old. He knew better. And at this point, this was a matter for his mother to deal with. And if she couldn't, then…then he'd just expel the boy. Maybe that would get Abigail Stolz's attention.

* * *

"Buggy!" Abigail's mother announced from the back door. "Babby! Buggy coming!"

"Are you expecting someone?" Abigail asked, walking away from the kitchen sink as she dried her hands on a towel, a red-and-white one with a rooster on it. It wasn't a Plain towel; it wasn't the kind most Amish women had in their homes. But her mother had spotted it at Spence's Bazaar the previous week and had made such a fuss about wanting it that Abigail's father had bought it for her.

"It's not Plain," Abigail had argued under her breath as they'd gotten into line to pay for it. "We're new to Hickory Grove still, *Dat*. What will our bishop think?"

"What will he think?" he had asked as he peeled off dollar bills from a wad in his pocket that he kept together with a rubber band from a bunch of bananas. "He'll think I'm a husband who indulges his wife once in a while. That's what he'll think."

"But it's red, *Daddi*," Abigail had murmured.

"That's why she likes it," he had whispered back with a smile.

Abigail walked to the back door and peered out the window. There actually *was* a buggy approaching. It was not one of her mother's false alarms. Abigail didn't recognize the horse, though. It was a pretty light brown, almost caramel shade. Not the color horse one often saw pulling an Amish buggy. "Cover your head, *Mam*," she instructed absently, still watching out the window.

June's hands flew to the tight bun of thin hair that had grayed long ago. "Where's my *kapp*, Babby? Someone's taken my *kapp*."

"No one's taken your *kapp*. You've put it somewhere and I can't find it. It's been missing since morning."

Abigail walked into the mudroom that was off the kitchen and grabbed a dark blue scarf from a rusty nail in the wall. Her father had finished a lot of work in the last eight months since he and Abigail's mother had bought the property, but there was still a lot to be done. One item on Abigail's lengthy to-do list was to add pegs to the walls in the mudroom that also served as a laundry room. It just seemed uncivilized to her, to be hanging coats and cloaks and hats on nails.

"I don't like that scarf," June fussed, trying to push her daughter's hands away as Abigail wrapped it neatly around her mother's head, covering her hair. For modesty's sake, no one but a woman's husband was supposed to see her bare head.

"I want the pink one," June fussed.

"We don't wear pink scarves, *Mam*." Abigail deftly tied the scarf at the nape of her mother's neck. "There you go." She smiled as she smoothed the fabric at her mother's forehead. "All done."

June King was a small woman, frail in appearance. But even though she was seventy years old, she was as strong as an ox, especially when she took a notion to put up a fight. Which was happening with more frequency, in Abigail's opinion. Her father, however, disagreed. He either downplayed his wife's inappropriate behavior and speech or denied it altogether. Abigail knew that deep in her father's heart, he must know his wife of fifty years was showing signs of dementia, but she suspected he wasn't yet ready to face the truth.

"Who's here, Babby?" June asked, as excited as a

young girl going to her first singing. "Do you think it's the bishop?"

"I don't know who it is. Maybe a neighbor," Abigail responded.

"I think it's the bishop."

"*Ne*, I think not." Abigail walked back across the kitchen to turn down the apple butter simmering on the stove. She'd found some apples no longer in their prime in the cellar and decided to do something with them before they spoiled. "Bishop Simon's driving horse is black."

Outside, Abigail's father's dog, Boots, began to bark. He was an old border collie, mostly deaf and suffering from arthritis, but he still managed to stand watch over the farm. When her parents had moved to Delaware the previous fall and taken the dog with them, Abigail's son had missed him dearly. When she and Jamie had arrived in Delaware, Jamie had been as excited to see the dog as his grandparents.

"Oh, my! It's that handsome schoolmaster!" June declared, clapping her hands. She pushed open the screen door and walked out onto the back porch, leaving the door wide open.

"The schoolmaster?" Immediately concerned, Abigail dropped the wooden spoon she'd been using to stir the apple butter onto the counter. It fell so hard that it bounced. "What's he doing here?" She glanced at the round, black-and-white battery-powered clock on the kitchen wall. It was only two forty-five. School wasn't out for another fifteen minutes.

Abigail hustled to the open back door, her heart fluttering in her chest. It had to be Jamie. Was he ill? Had he injured? She fought the panic rising in her chest as she went down the porch steps and into the driveway, walking past her mother.

"Schoolteacher!" June greeted, waving eagerly. "So glad you could stop by. Come in for coffee and apple streusel! My daughter makes a fine streusel!"

"*Mam*, shush," Abigail murmured. "It's not proper calling out to a man like that."

Now that the buggy was closer, Abigail could see that it was indeed the schoolmaster. And her Jamie. She could see her little boy through the buggy's windshield. He didn't look ill, or injured, but why else would the teacher be bringing him home in his buggy? And early, no less.

Abigail hurried out into the middle of the driveway, catching the pretty mare's halter as the buggy rolled to a stop. Boots barked and ran in circles around the conveyance.

Abigail went straightaway to the passenger's side and slid open the door. "Jamie? Are you all right?" she asked, trying as best she could to hide her alarm. "What's wrong, *sohn*?" She reached out to him to take him in her arms. He was really too big for her to carry anymore, or even hold in her lap. And he didn't like it. But Jamie was her baby boy, her only child. A mother couldn't be criticized for caring about her child, could she?

"I'm all right," Jamie said, pushing his mother away. "I'm fine. I can get down myself."

Abigail clasped his cheeks between her hands, looking into his brown eyes. He *looked* fine. Not sick at all. "Not hurt?" she asked.

"Not hurt or sick," the schoolmaster said dryly, pulling the brake on the buggy.

His name was Ethan Miller. Abigail had met him several times. They were part of the same church district. The schoolmaster had also stopped by the house a couple of times as he walked home from school—to complain about her son's behavior. She didn't care for Ethan Miller. He was grumpy and he expected too much of Jamie too soon. The poor boy had just moved halfway across the country. His life had been turned upside down like an apple cart: leaving his friends in Wisconsin, living with his grandparents, joining a new community. Who could expect there wouldn't be a few bumps in the road?

The schoolmaster got out of the buggy and walked around to Abigail. He was a tall man, slender, with blond hair, brown eyes and a carefully trimmed beard. Some might have thought him handsome, and maybe in other circumstances, she might have, too.

The border collie sniffed at the schoolmaster's heels and then wandered away.

"I brought Jamie home because we had a problem at school today," the schoolmaster said. *"Again."*

Abigail looked down at her son who was now standing beside her. "Go into the house with your *gross-mami*," she told him, stroking his shoulder. "She'll find you a snack."

Jamie smiled up at her. *"Ya, Mam."*

"I'm not making him a snack, Babby," her mother put in. She was standing on the far side of the driveway, but she had heard every word. Abigail's father was losing his hearing but her mother's was as good as her own and it seemed as if she never missed a thing. "Jamie's been naughty. I don't make snacks for naughty boys."

The schoolmaster glanced June's way and then returned his gaze to Abigail. "Actually, I'd like Jamie to stay here. And tell you for himself what he did."

Abigail looked at her son, then at the schoolmaster. "I don't understand."

When the teacher didn't say anything, she turned her stare back to Jamie. "What did you do?"

"I didn't mean to, *Mam*," Jamie said, pouting. "I'm very hungry. Could I have my snack?"

"Tell her," the schoolmaster said, using a tone of voice that Abigail didn't much care for. Who did he think he was, speaking to a young boy so harshly?

"Please, *Mam*?" Jamie whined. "I'm so hungry." He touched his forehead. "I'm feeling dizzy."

"Tell her," the schoolmaster repeated, lowering his voice until it was little more than a rumble.

"Tell her, you naughty boy!" June called from the other side of the driveway.

Jamie's eyes filled with tears. "I tried to tip over the girls' outhouse. I just wanted to see if I could do it." The words tumbled out of his mouth. "I was trying to use a lever. Like *Grossdadi* taught me. I didn't know Elsie was inside! I didn't want to hurt anyone."

Abigail's eyes widened. "You tried to tip over an outhouse? With someone inside?"

He grabbed the hem of her apron. "I didn't mean to, *Mam*!"

"There, there," Abigail soothed, stroking his blond curly head. "It's all right."

"It's *not* all right," the schoolmaster said. Now he was taking on a tone with *her*. "It was dangerous, what he did. Then he lied to me and when he finally *did* admit what he'd done, he wasn't even apologetic."

"I am sorry, *Mam*! I am," her son cried into her apron.

"He says he sorry," Abigail returned stiffly, meeting the schoolmaster's gaze.

"He's not sorry he did it. He's sorry he got caught." The schoolmaster brought his hand to his neatly trimmed beard and stroked it. "And that's not good enough, Abigail."

"Oh it isn't, *Ethan*? For whom?" She let go of Jamie to take a step closer to the schoolmaster. Her irritation was rising by the second. Her father had always said her quick temper was her worst trait, but sometimes she thought maybe it was her best. Life had been hard as a single woman since her husband's death and it had been her experience that sometimes standing up to men got things done when nothing else would.

"That's bad, tipping over outhouses," June put in from the far side of the driveway.

Ethan stood there in front of Abigail for a moment. He glanced away, then back at her. Maybe he had realized that she wasn't a weak-minded woman who could be pushed around by any man who wanted to give her advice on how to raise her son.

"This is the *fourth* time I've had to speak with you about Jamie's behavior at school," Ethan intoned, "and I'm ready to just ex—" He took a breath and glanced at her son. "Go with your grandmother," he said quietly.

Jamie took off for the house and Ethan met Abigail's gaze.

For some reason, his soft tone made her angrier than if he had just raised his voice to her. And who did he think he was to be ordering her son around after school hours? "You're ready to just what?" she demanded.

"Expel him," he answered flatly.

"Expel? *Expel* him?" Abigail sputtered.

"In my day, boys were paddled," June called. "That's what my *dat* did when my brothers were bad. A good switching is what this boy needs, Babby."

Abigail whipped around to her mother. "*Mam*, please see to your grandson. *Inside*." She turned back to the schoolmaster.

"You've left me with little other choice. If Jamie's behavior doesn't improve, he's out," Ethan said. "I've asked you *repeatedly* to rein your son in and so far, I've seen no improvement. He doesn't turn in his school-work, or when he does it's not complete. He doesn't listen," Ethan said, ticking off on his fingers. "He's disruptive, disrespectful and out of control."

"*Out of control?* He's nine years old!" Abigail pointed toward the house in the direction Jamie had just gone. "And what does that say of you, Ethan?" She placed her hands on her hips. "A teacher who can't control one little mischievous boy?"

"*Mischievous?*" Ethan flared. "*Ne*, his behavior is beyond mischievous. What about last week when he cut the strings off Martha's prayer *kapp* with scissors? What of the cow pie he put in Johnny Fisher's bologna sandwich? What about—"

"You know what I have a mind to do, Ethan Miller," Abigail interrupted, gritting her teeth.

Ethan rested his hands on his hips. "What?" he demanded.

"I have a mind to go to the school board and have you dismissed."

He laughed, which made her even angrier. If that was possible.

"Dismissed under what grounds?" Ethan scoffed.

"On your lack of control in the classroom," she told

him. She folded her arms over her chest. "What kind of teacher are you that little boys can get away with such things? It's clear to me that you are unable to control your students and that…that you should be replaced immediately because you—" she pointed at him "—are obviously not doing your job."

"*My job* is not to teach your child how to behave." He pointed back at her. "That is *your* job. It's obvious the boy needs discipline at home."

Abigail drew back, dropping her arms to her sides. Somewhere in the very back of her mind, she knew he had a point, but he had made her so angry that she couldn't think straight.

Ethan walked away. "Get your son under control or I'm expelling him," he warned.

"I certainly hope you don't speak to your wife with that tone," she flung back at him.

Without another word, the schoolmaster got into his buggy, turned around in the driveway and headed out the way he'd come. Abigail watched him until he was halfway down the lane and then marched toward the house. Who did Ethan Miller think he was? How dare he threaten to expel her son! She passed her mother who was still standing there beside the driveway.

June watched her daughter walk by. "What do you think of the schoolteacher, Babby?" she asked brightly.

"Me?" She broke into a broad smile, not giving Abigail a chance to respond. "I *like* him."

Chapter Two

Ethan took his time seeing to Butterscotch, leading her to the water trough and then giving her a good brushing until her coat gleamed. Afterward, he fed her a scoop of oats and set her loose in the pasture to graze until sunset when he'd put her up in the barn for the night. He knew it was foolish, but the time he spent with the mare made him feel closer to his wife, more than five years gone now. Closer to her in memory at least. How she'd loved the mare, their little farm in upstate New York, their quiet life. How she had loved him.

He'd been so lost after her unexpected death that he thought he might die of his grief. He didn't, of course, just as his wise father had predicted. And as the days turned into months, then years, though he hadn't stopped loving her, the pain was no longer so sharp. Now, after so much time had passed, more often than not, he smiled when he thought her, rather than cried.

Ethan stood beside the gate and watched Butterscotch wander off to graze in a bed of fresh, flowering clover. Then, his hands deep in his pockets, he walked down the lane toward the harness shop in search of his father. He was still mulling over his conversation with Abigail Stolz. He was hoping to talk with his father about Jamie and the boy's mother. Maybe he could offer a different perspective.

Ethan took his time walking, taking in the two-hundred-acre farm, its fields that were now turning green, white fencing, barns and outbuildings. In the two years since the family had moved to Hickory Grove from New York, Millers' shop had flourished. Despite the local competition of Troyer's just three miles away, his father had found ways to provide goods and services to both Amish and Englisher customers. Not only did he repair and make nearly any kind of leatherwork, but he also sold the type of supplies a man with livestock needed: liniments, wormers, fly and pest control traps and sprays, you name it. And that wasn't all he was selling these days.

A year ago, Ethan's stepsister Bay Laurel, who they called Bay, had started selling jams and jellies, fresh eggs, preserves, and baked goods. Her single shelf had turned into an entire aisle and his father was considering expanding the size of the store to keep up with the women's side of the business. Then there was Ethan's brother Joshua, newly wed, who had built a greenhouse over the winter and was about to open a business selling seedlings, flowers and vegetable plants.

All that, and Benjamin, his father, was still dreaming of expanding his business inside the huge dairy barn he'd remodeled. He wanted to go into buggy making. Ethan wasn't much for working in the harness shop. That was why he had taken the job of schoolmaster when the position had become vacant. But buggy making was quickly becoming a passion of his. He still had a lot to learn, but he liked using his hands to make a wheel, a door, a padded seat. Alone in the shop, or even working beside his father, he loved the peacefulness of it. No little girls squirming in their seats, no little boys bringing toads into the schoolhouse. No Jamie Stoltz trying to tip over an outhouse.

Ethan's annoyance with the boy came back in a single breath. Which turned to near anger toward the mother. He felt sorry for Abigail, a widow alone trying to raise a boy without a father, but surely she understood that it was her duty to control the boy's behavior. Ethan couldn't help thinking that if Jamie was bad at school, it was likely he wasn't all that well behaved at home either. He got that impression from the grandmother. He couldn't remember her name, though they'd been introduced at church. Daniel King, Abigail's father, and his wife had been in the harness shop a couple of times and they'd bumped into each other at a dinner celebrating Epiphany back in January. That was just before Abigail and her son had arrived in Hickory Grove. He had heard from his stepsister Ginger that she was widowed three or four years ago, though Ginger hadn't known any of the details. That fact alone gave him good reason not to judge the woman so quickly, but—

"Ethan? You okay?"

He looked up. He'd been so lost in his thoughts that he hadn't seen or even heard his sister-in-law, Phoebe, approaching.

"I thought you were going to walk right by me." She met his gaze with a smile. She was wearing a blue scarf tied around her head and the denim coat one of his stepsisters had commandeered. Ordinarily, Amish women didn't wear men's denim barn coats, even around their house, but there was nothing ordinary about his step-mother's girls. Or his brother Joshua's new wife.

"Uh, sorry, just thinking. *Ya*, I'm fine," he said. He liked Phoebe. She'd come from a hard life, bringing a little boy with her, but she'd managed to make a new life there in Hickory Grove. She was sweet and kind and fun, but the thing Ethan liked most about her was her resilience. He admired her ability to see beyond her troubles and find the goodness in the world God provided. He was beginning to think maybe he needed to take a page from her book. As much as he hated to admit that his father and stepmother, Rosemary, were right, it *was* time to move on with his life. He knew it was what his Mary would want. But he just… So far, he just hadn't been able to get there.

"Been down to the mailbox," Phoebe said. She held up a bundle of flyers and envelopes. "Something here for you. A bank statement, I think." She stopped in front of him, sifting through the pile in her arms. With a family their size—his father and stepmother, his stepsisters, stepbrothers, and brothers still living at home, as well as Phoebe and her son—they numbered fifteen at the supper table. And that was if his stepsister Lovey and her family didn't join them. They received a lot of mail.

"It's here somewhere," she said, still thumbing through the stack.

"Just leave it on the counter," he told her, turning so he was still facing her, backing down the driveway, hands deep in his pants pockets. "Have you seen my *dat*?"

"In the shop. In the back, I think. I stopped to see Ginger on the way to the mailbox. She's working the register."

He nodded, turned and continued on his way.

"See you for supper," Phoebe called after him.

His back now to her, he raised his hand in response.

Ethan found Ginger occupied at the register ringing up an English woman. "My *dat*?"

She nodded over her shoulder as she dropped fly paper into a brown paper bag. "Back in the buggy shop, I think. UPS delivered leather for seat covers."

Ethan went through the swinging half door to get behind the counter, then through the next door and into the leather workshop. He nodded to his brother Jacob who was busy with an awl punching holes in what looked to be a new bridle he was making. Beside him, seated on a stool, was their eleven-year-old stepbrother, Jesse, who was talking a mile a minute about a bass in their pond he was set on catching.

Ethan walked through the shop and into a hall where the newly constructed walls had drywall but no paint yet. Doorway cuts in the walls led to empty space now that could be turned into additional workrooms or an office if his father wanted to expand later. At the end of the hall, he found the door to the buggy shop open.

Benjamin Miller's door was always open, figuratively and literally, and not just to his wife and children and stepchildren, but to his community, as well. He was a good listener, but he also didn't hesitate to give his opinion if it was asked. His father was the wisest man Ethan knew and even though he had just had his thirty-third birthday, he was still young enough to need his father's guidance occasionally. Old enough to know it.

Benjamin turned on the stool where he sat at his workbench and peered over the glasses he wore for up close work. "Get that stovepipe?"

Ethan shook his head. "Didn't make it to Byler's. Had a problem with one of my students. Had to take him home. I'll go get the stovepipe tomorrow."

"Whenever you get to it will be fine." Benjamin looked up at his eldest son, reading glasses perched on his nose. In his fifties, he was a heavyset man with a reddish beard that was going gray, a square chin and a broad nose. Ethan had his father's brown eyes, but his mother's tall, slender frame.

"I'm hoping this break in the weather means we won't be needing to light that old woodstove 'til fall," his father went on, nodding in the direction of the stove they'd recently installed. His father had traded a new full harness for the stove with a man from over in Rose Valley. Benjamin liked bartering and did it whenever he could. He said it reminded him of his childhood back in Canada where he'd grown up. In those days, he said, paper money was rarely exchanged; a checking account was unheard of. The sizable Amish community relied mostly on themselves and traded for everything.

Benjamin turned back to the piece of paper he was studying on his workbench: a sketch of the buggy he and Ethan were building together. It was a small, open buggy, referred to sometimes as a courting buggy. "You said you had a problem with a student. Get it worked out?"

Ethan took a deep breath. He sighed, removed his wide-brimmed straw hat and ran his fingers through his blond hair. His gaze settled on the box on the cement floor that had been opened to reveal yards of leather they would use to upholster the new buggy's seat. "*Ne...* Well, maybe. I don't know."

Benjamin removed his glasses. "Want to talk about it?"

Ethan sighed again, and then the whole story just came out. It wasn't the first time he'd talked to his father about Jamie. He knew the boy had been a problem since he'd arrived at school, but still, he listened patiently, commenting or urging Ethan on as he relayed the most recent incident.

When Ethan was done, he dropped down on a stool near the door. "I've just had it, *Dat*. I've half a mind to—" He halted and then started again. "I've half a mind to resign, effective the end of the school year. If I give the school board notice now, they'll have time to find another teacher by September."

"That what you want to do? Quit teaching?"

Ethan set his hat on his knee, studying the courting buggy that was nearly complete. The project was so close to being done that Benjamin was already working on the plans for a more traditional family-sized buggy. "I don't know, *Dat*. I'm thinking maybe there's some truth to what Abigail said. Maybe I'm not cut from the cloth of a schoolmaster."

"Not sure I agree with that. Other folks in Hickory Grove would say you're the best teacher they've had for their children. Last Saturday over at the mill, John Fisher was talking about inviting some other Amish teachers—men and women—to our schoolhouse for a day for you to run some kind of training. To get teachers together to talk about ways to teach our children about the world we live in these days. It's not like in my day when we were isolated from Englishers. Insulated. No denying that as the world has changed, we've been forced to change. But that doesn't mean we have to give up who we are. That means we've got to deal with the changes not just in our homes and our church, but our schools, too. Men like you, you understand that. You understand how hard it can be for our children. To hear the music, see the behavior and not covet it."

Ethan worried his lower lip, thinking. Everything his father said was true. Teaching school wasn't easy, not with Amish kids being exposed to Englishers: the clothes, the cars, the behavior. You couldn't keep young folks on the farm all the time so they had to know how to deal with the world they were supposed to stand apart from. He knew they needed to be guided in how to stay on the path their ancestors had set out for them and school was one of the places they could find that guidance.

What Ethan didn't know was if he was really the one to be doing it.

"That said," his father went on, "if you do decide teaching isn't your calling, you know you can join me here." He gestured to the workshop they were both proud of. "Before you know it, Levi will be home and we'll be getting serious about production."

Over the winter they'd added an overhead door in the shop big enough to accommodate a buggy, and they purchased quite a few tools. A buggy maker had to be a welder, an upholsterer, a carpenter, mechanic and painter all rolled into one and he needed different tools for each aspect of the construction. Ethan's brother Levi was staying with friends in Lancaster, Pennsylvania, apprenticing as a buggy maker. His plan was to learn what he could over the next year or so and then return to Hickory Grove. At least that's why he said he'd moved to Lancaster, though Ethan suspected it was the larger population of single women that had attracted him to accept the position.

Ethan eyed his father. "You think we're ready to go into business, do you? So far, we've just made that new family buggy for ourselves and the one for Lovey and Marshall."

"And your courting buggy is nearly done." Benjamin smiled, pointing at the sleek black buggy that took up the center of the shop.

Ethan shook his head. "Not mine. Will and Levi would get more use of it. Jacob. Before you know, Jesse will be taking girls home from singings."

Benjamin hesitated. "I know you don't want to hear this—"

Ethan held up his hand. *"Dat—"*

"I know you don't want to hear it but I'm going to say it anyway." He got off his stool and walked toward Ethan. "Because it's my duty as your father to say things you don't want to hear."

Ethan rose, clamping his hat down on his head.

"It's time for you to marry again, *sohn.*"

Ethan shook his head, surprised by the emotion that rose up in his throat, threatening to prevent him from speaking. He took a moment. *"Dat,"* he said when he found his voice. "We've been over this a hundred times. I don't know that I'll marry again." He stared at a spot on the floor, embarrassed by the feelings welling up in him. His father was never one to tell his sons it was wrong to show emotion. Benjamin Miller was an emotional man, Ethan's brother Joshua, too. But Ethan wasn't like them. He didn't know what to do with his sadness, his loneliness, except tamp it down, close it off, stay one step ahead of it.

"You need to find yourself a nice young woman, marry, have children."

Ethan stood there, unable to meet his father's gaze.

Benjamin smoothed the straps of his suspenders and then went on. "You join me in the shop and we'll start making buggies not just for family and neighbors but we'll take orders from Pennsylvania, Ohio, Kentucky, even. Rosemary's cousin in Kentucky says that when we're ready, he'll be the first one to put cash on our workbench. He's running a buggy that was his grandfather's because there's no one making them down there."

Benjamin took a step toward Ethan. "I'm not getting any younger, you know. Rosemary and I, we've talked about building a smaller house here on the property. Once you older boys are married, and Rosemary's girls, we'll have no need for such a big house. You marry and start having little ones and the big house is yours. Someday I'll be gone and this farm, this family, will be yours. Now, you know I've got things worked out so you and all your brothers will have a piece of it, but you'll be the head of this family someday—you'll be here to father your little brothers should I pass before they're full grown men."

"Dat," Ethan murmured.

"Sohn, it's what God means us to do. A man is to marry. And to marry, you have to get out there and meet a woman, court a woman."

Ethan closed his eyes, beginning to regret having come to his father. After the day he'd had, he didn't need a lecture. *"Dat*, even if I did have a notion to court a woman, who would that be?"

"Plenty of single young women in Hickory Grove," Benjamin declared, gesturing with his hands.

"Young. Exactly. Can you imagine me with one of

Ginger's or Nettie's friends?" Ethan lifted his gaze to meet his father's.

Benjamin shrugged. "So you want a more mature woman. A little harder to find, but they're around. There's that niece of Eunice's who stays with them sometimes. Dottie? She's not much to look at, but she's a woman of faith."

Ethan almost smiled. He knew Eunice Gruber's niece Dottie, one of the many nieces the woman paraded in front of the single men of Hickory Grove and he knew her well enough to know Dottie wasn't the kind he would court. It wasn't her looks that he cared about. He truly believed that beauty was in the eye of the beholder. It was Dottie's incessant giggling that bothered him. She might have been a woman over thirty, but she acted more like she was fourteen.

"I don't think Dottie is my type, *Dat*."

"Fine." He threw up his hands. "What about Abigail Stoltz? Nice-looking woman. She lost her husband. She understands what it's like to be alone, to—"

"Abigail?" Ethan demanded, almost laughing out loud. *"Dat*, did you not hear anything I said? She accused me of doing my job poorly. She threatened to have me *fired*." He shook his head adamantly. "I can guarantee you that if I took a mind to court a woman, she'd be the last one I'd pursue." He turned toward the door. "I need to move hay before supper. We're short in the barn."

"Just think on what I said," Benjamin called after him.

I'll think on it all right, Ethan said to himself as he walked out the door. Now he was as frustrated with his father as he was with Abigail.

* * *

"Amen," Daniel King announced heartily as he drew silent grace to an end. He clasped his calloused hands together, looking across the kitchen table at Abigail. He was plump to his wife's slenderness, his gray hair cut short in a bowl cut, his beard long and gray. His gray eyes twinkled with kindness when he spoke. "Looks good, *dochder*. Let's eat. I did a little plowing in the garden this afternoon and I'm hungry enough to eat this table."

Jamie giggled. "You can't eat a table, *Grossdadi*. You'd get splinters in your mouth. Knock out some teeth."

"Only if the teeth were loose." Daniel tousled his grandson's blond hair. "Like yours."

"Just this one." Jamie wiggled one of his front teeth with his fingers.

"Not at the table," Abigail chastised as she put a pork chop smothered in gravy and onions on her mother's plate and then her son's. She passed the serving dish to her father.

"I knew a boy who once ate a table," June said, heaping cinnamon applesauce onto her plate. "A big supper table we used to use for church dinners. Ten feet, I suspect. Chewed the boards to sawdust and had nary a splinter to swallow."

Jamie cut his eyes at his mother but didn't contradict his grandmother. Instead, he began scooping the gravy and onions off his pork chop and dumping them on his mother's empty plate.

Abigail gave her mother and her son a serving of mashed potatoes, then passed the bowl to her father. "More gravy on the stove if anyone wants some." She glanced at her mother who was now spooning apple-sauce onto her pork chop. She rested her hand on her mother's for a moment. "You won't like that, *Mam*," she said quietly.

"I like it," June declared loudly. "They're dry." She dumped another spoonful on her pork chop.

"They're not dry, wife," Daniel put in, adding pats of fresh homemade butter to his potatoes. "Abby makes a fine pork chop."

"Dry as the boards in that table that boy Israel ate." June began putting applesauce on top of her mashed potatoes.

Abigail gently took the Ball jar of applesauce from her mother and served her son.

"Not near the potatoes!" Jamie complained, laying his hand across his plate.

"My day," Daniel said good-naturedly as he took the quart of applesauce from his daughter, "a boy ate what his mother put on his plate. That or he put his own food on his plate. You're old enough to get your own pork chop, boy."

Abigail tried to spoon green beans onto Jamie's plate, but he held out his hand to her.

"I don't like green beans. No green beans."

"I'm only giving you three. You can well eat three measly green beans," she said, irritation creeping into her voice. She wasn't upset with Jamie, of course. It was his teacher. It was Ethan Miller who had her struggling to control her exasperation and think of him with kindness in her heart. She'd been stewing over him since he'd brought Jamie home. She still couldn't believe the nerve he had to come there and try to tell her how she should raise her son.

"You don't like green beans with bacon?" Daniel scoffed. He took the serving bowl from Abigail. "Suits me just fine. More for me." He put a healthy portion on his plate and then a smaller one on his wife's. "Saw that the teacher brought Jamie home. Spotted that dun of his from the garden," he remarked, directing his comment to Abigail. "My grandson in trouble again?"

Abigail took a moment to gather her thoughts before she responded. She and her father got along well, but like all parents and adult children, especially those living together, they had their disagreements.

He had a lot to say about how she was raising her son, and much of it critical. He thought she coddled Jamie, that he was immature and that she expected too little of her boy. He'd actually used the word *discipline* the other day, the same word Ethan had used, which had annoyed her all the more. Men didn't understand the relationship between a woman and her only son. And neither knew what it was like to lose a spouse, to be raising a child alone.

Abigail stalled, using the time to cut up Jamie's pork chop for him as she chose her words carefully. "There was an incident at school today. Ethan wanted to talk with me about it."

"Naughty boy," June chastised, shaking her fork at her grandson.

Abigail pushed Jamie's plate back to him and began to serve herself helpings of the green beans, pork chops and potatoes. Then, suddenly remembering that she had buttermilk biscuits in the oven, she rose from her chair. "Oh, goodness. The biscuits. I don't think that pesky timer is working." She hurried for the stove, grabbing a hot mitt off the counter.

"What'd you do, Jamie?" Abigail's father asked.

As Abigail opened the oven, she glanced over her shoulder, waiting to hear what her son would say.

Jamie stared at his supper plate, his hands clasping it. "The kids are mean to me. They don't want to play with me at recess." He stuck out his lower lip. "I want to go home to Maple Shade."

"Oh, Jamie, you know that's not possible." Abigail pulled the pan of biscuits from the oven. Luckily, she'd caught them before they began to burn. "We sold our farm, remember? We live with your grandmother and grandfather now. We came to help them with the farm."

"What did you do?" her father repeated, putting a forkful of mashed potatoes into his mouth. "Mmm. Just like I like them. Lots of pepper." He eyed his grandson as he chewed and waited.

After a long moment of silence, Abigail said, "The schoolmaster said—"

"Daughter, let my grandson tell me. He can speak. He has a mouth."

"Oh, you're in trouble now," June said quietly. She reached for the jar of applesauce again.

Abigail dumped the pan of biscuits onto a plate and carried them to the table. "You have to eat something besides applesauce, *Mam*." She set the biscuits in the middle of the table and put one on her plate.

"He's in trouble," June responded, pointing at Jamie with a serving spoon that was heaped with applesauce. "That handsome schoolteacher brought him home because he tipped over the outhouse, girl inside." She plopped more applesauce on top of her potatoes.

"He didn't knock it over." Abigail gently took the spoon and the jar from her mother's hands and then slid into her chair. "Go on," she encouraged. "Tell your granddad what you did."

The boy pressed his lips together, slowly looking up. "I was trying to make a lever. Like you showed me at the barn the other day when you were trying to get the cardboard under the rain barrel. I wanted to see if it would work."

Abigail's father met her gaze but he held his tongue, though only until supper was over and Jamie had been excused. The boy took no time at all to race from the kitchen and out the back door, headed for the barn he said, to feed the cats.

"So the schoolteacher had to bring him home this time?" Daniel intoned as he carried a stack of dirty dishes to the sink. "Because of his behavior?"

June had taken her position at the sink to wash. It was a chore she could still do well, and she liked it. Abigail had taken over most of the cooking, but she let her mother wash dishes, understanding that it was important that she still contribute to the household.

"Wasn't there a problem last week?" Abigail's father pressed when she didn't respond.

Abigail carried the leftover biscuits, covered in a clean dishtowel, to the pie safe. "Jamie told me he didn't know Elsie was inside when he started rocking the outhouse."

Daniel left the stack of dirty dishes on the counter and went back to gather more. "You believe him?"

Abigail hesitated as she tried to puzzle out her thoughts. She had caught Jamie in a few fibs from time to time, but she didn't want to believe he'd intentionally risk injuring someone and then lie to cover it up. Ethan believed Jamie *had* known the little girl was inside, which would mean Jamie had lied. Abigail didn't think Ethan would make up such a thing...which meant her son had told them an untruth. She had to face it.

"He's having a hard time, *Dat*. He misses his home, his friends. He still misses his *dat*."

"But didn't you tell me he was having trouble in school *before* you moved here? Not getting along with the other children, not doing his lessons. Wasn't that one of the reasons why you decided not to stay in Wisconsin until the end of the school year?"

Abigail closed the pie safe and just stood there for a moment. Her stomach was in knots. She'd barely eaten. She didn't know what to say to her father. She didn't know what to do to help her son. She turned slowly to face him. "It's a hard age."

"He could have hurt that girl."

Abigail took a handful of dirty eating utensils from her father's hand. "I understand that. And I'm going to talk to him."

Her father stood there looking down at her. She knew he had more to say on the matter, but thankfully, he didn't. Instead, he said quietly, "I want to help you, daughter. I want to help Jamie. He's the only grandson I have."

"I know you do." She squeezed his arm. "Why don't you go out and finish up your chores. *Mam* and I can take care of the dishes." She shrugged. "Maybe take Jamie fishing in the pond for a little while? He loves fishing with you."

Daniel nodded. "I can do that." He turned to go, then back to her. "But you know this isn't just going to right itself on its own, don't you? It's only going to get worse. Something has to change. You keep doing the same thing and it doesn't work, you have to change your approach."

"I'll talk to him, *Dat*." Abigail bit down on her lower lip. "And I'll think on it. Figure out what I need to do differently." Her thoughts immediately returned to her conversation with Ethan. He'd threatened to expel Jamie. She couldn't let that happen. Schooling was too necessary, and she knew she couldn't teach him at home, not with the house and her mother to deal with.

She closed her eyes for a moment, listening to her father's footsteps as he left the kitchen. She had been feeling overwhelmed for weeks. She had hoped that being here would make things easier for her and Jamie. She'd thought a change of scenery might help Jamie at school, but obviously, she'd been wrong. Her first impulse had been to blame the schoolteacher, but now she felt bad. He was just doing his job. And she'd lashed out at him. She'd raised her voice.

And now she owed him an apology. She just wasn't sure how to go about it.

Chapter Three

It turned out that the opportunity to speak to Ethan presented itself quickly enough. The following afternoon, Abigail was visited by Karl Lapp whose property adjoined her father's. He'd caught Jamie, who'd been on his way home from school, trying to "ride" one of his cows. One about to give birth. She'd made Jamie apologize to Karl and then as punishment, she told her son she would be walking him to and from school for the rest of the week.

"You can't walk me to the door," Jamie whined the next morning as he and Abigail turned into the driveway to the white clapboard schoolhouse. "The kids will see you. They'll make fun of me."

Abigail drew her heavy cloak closer. Even though the grass was beginning to turn green and the trees to blossom, it was still chilly in the mornings. She lifted her face to feel the morning sun, enjoying its heat and the promise of a new day. The sunshine brought her hope, hope that her mother would have a good day mentally, that Jamie's behavior would improve and that she wouldn't feel quite so lonely in the world. Certainly, she had her mother and father and son, and she was thankful for them. But there was an ache in her heart where her husband, Egan, had once been. She still missed him every day. Mourned him every day.

"Mam?" Jamie tugged at his mother's cloak, getting her attention. "Did you hear what I said? Someone's going to see you."

"We're early enough that I doubt it. Unless I *want* them to see me," she added looking at him sternly, hoping he would read it as a warning. She shifted the basket she carried on her arm. Inside was a peace offering of sorts for the schoolmaster. "Unless Karl catches you on one of his cows again. Then I might decide to come to school with you every day. I'll sit beside you and help you with your lessons."

"Please, no," Jamie groaned. "I won't do it again." He kicked a piece of gravel in the driveway. "I was just bored is all. It's a long walk home. That's why I went to look at the cows."

"It wasn't the looking that got you into trouble." When he didn't say anything, she went on. "You know how I feel about saying you're bored. There's always work you can do around the house. And it's a mile from here home so I don't want to hear it. When I was your age, I walked four miles to school each day. Then four miles home." She hooked her thumb over her back.

"No one here walks. All the kids have a push scooter," he complained.

"Not *everyone* has a scooter," she countered. The gravel crunched under her sneakers. "I see boys and girls walking past our place on the way to school every morning."

He bounced up and down on the toes of his boots. He was growing so fast that she'd had to buy them new just before they left Wisconsin. Being her only child, and having no family nearby, there were no hand-me-downs. Everything had to be made or bought new.

"But I *want* a scooter."

"Don't whine, *sohn*. You're not a *boppli* anymore. And maybe you *can* have one. When your behavior is better." She walked up the steps to open the door to the schoolhouse. "When you're doing better with your lessons."

He stood at the bottom of the stairs to the schoolhouse and looked up at her. "You're not coming inside, are you?" he groaned.

"I am." She walked through the doorway and into the small coatroom. One long wall was lined with hooks for coats and bonnets and such, the other with windows. "I need to talk to your teacher for a minute." She handed Jamie his lunch pail.

"It goes up there." He pointed at shelves built on the wall across from the entrance.

"Then you should probably put it there." She eyed him in a way that she hoped would be reprimanding, and he scuffed his feet across the floor toward the shelving. She tapped on the inner door that led into the one-room schoolhouse and opened it.

Ethan didn't glance up from a large wooden desk at the far end of the room. The schoolhouse looked little different than the one she'd attended as a girl back in Wisconsin. The single room was square with plenty of windows on the opposite walls so they would get a good breeze in the warmer months. A large wood-stove with a stovepipe going up through the roof in the center of the room was cold but would put out plenty of heat in the winter. There was the teacher's desk at the head of the room with a green chalkboard behind it. The remainder of the space was filled with wooden desks and chairs. The only difference she saw from her school days was that instead of lining the desks and chairs in rows facing the blackboard, the desks were pushed together to form groups. Some had as many as eight desks together, some had as few as two.

Abigail halted a few steps inside the door. The schoolmaster still hadn't looked up at her so she could study him unnoticed. Her mother kept calling him the handsome schoolteacher, which annoyed her because… well, because *he* annoyed her. But also because she did find him handsome in a married schoolteacher way.

She cleared her throat.

He looked up. "Abigail." He didn't smile.

She pressed her lips together having second thoughts about coming there. About preparing the lunch for him she carried in her basket. She'd made it because Jamie had told her, in passing, that most days his teacher didn't get to eat his lunch. He was always giving it to a student for one reason or another. Jamie told her that the previous day, Mary Fisher had left hers at home on her kitchen table. Mary had eaten the teacher's pork chop sandwich, his potato chips and peach cobbler. He'd had water from the pump outside.

"Ethan." She nodded, forcing a quick smile that came as fast as it went.

He rose from his chair, setting a red ink pen on his desk. Her son disliked his red pen and the marks in the form of an X Ethan made on his math papers. "Where's Jamie?" he asked.

"Hiding, I think." She nodded in the direction of the cloakroom.

"From me?" He came around the big red oak desk that had to be fifty years old if not older.

"From both of us, I think."

"You walked him to school. Because of the incident yesterday with Karl's cows?" He leaned against the desk, crossing his arms over his chest. He had on the same clothes every Amish man in Kent County wore, denim trousers, suspenders and a long-sleeved colored shirt. His was a pale green, faded with years of laundering, but unblemished by rips or tears. On his feet, he wore a pair of black athletic sneakers.

She glanced down at her own sneakers that were similar to his though hers were blue. "How did you hear? It was just yesterday." She looked up at him.

"Amish telegraph." The corners of his mouth turned up ever so slightly. "That's what my stepmother likes to call it. Let's see…" He raised his thumb, counting. "Karl's wife, Bitty, told Mary Fisher's mother, Edna." He held up his forefinger. "Who told my stepsister Lovey's grandmother Lynita, who told Eunice Gruber." He added two more fingers. "Who then told all of the women at the less-than-ten-items checkout register at Byler's store." He started counting on his other hand. "Who included my stepmother, Rosemary, and her friend Hannah Hartman." He dropped both hands. "And Eunice, I have to warn you, has probably told every Amish woman in Hickory Grove by this morning. By tonight, I suspect the entire county will know. I give it a week to reach my great-aunt in Michigan."

Abigail, unable to help herself, chuckled. It had been the same way in Maple Shade, Wisconsin, where she'd come from. The women didn't have telephones of course, but there was always gossip to be had. And it traveled fast. Sometimes the subject was the antics of a naughty boy or the details of someone's cousin coming to visit after a betrothal breakup. But the good thing about the Amish telegraph was that the moment a member of the community was hurt or injured, or just needed a kind word, that was also shared, allowing the women to always be there for each other. And truth be told, the men gossiped, too; they were just less open about it.

"Jamie won't be riding anyone else's cows," Abigail told Ethan. "He's promised. And as punishment, I'll be walking him to and from school the rest of the week."

"Good thinking." Ethan lifted an eyebrow, nodding in approval. "Nothing a boy his age hates more than having his *mammi* walk him to school."

They were both quiet for a moment. Awkwardly quiet. Then Abigail spoke up, her gaze fixed on the old floorboards. "I… I wanted to apologize for the other day. What I said about going to the school board about you. It's only that… I was upset." When Ethan didn't respond, she glanced up at him.

He was watching her. After another stretch of silence that seemed to go on for days rather than seconds, he said, "I understand. Parents. Children. It's complicated."

The sound of children's voices came from the cloakroom. Students were beginning to arrive, which was a relief because now that Abigail had made her apology, she didn't have to stand here and talk to Ethan any longer. Just because she'd apologized didn't mean she approved of the way he was handling Jamie. And she didn't have time to dawdle anyway. She had chores waiting for her. It was Wednesday, which meant she had piles of dirty laundry to be washed and hung to dry on the line. She'd already hung a load of sheets and left the washer running. She had wet trousers and shirts waiting for her. "I... I packed a lunch for you."

"Lunch?" He looked at her questioningly. "I brought a lunch."

"I know, but... But Jamie said you don't always get to eat it." She handed him the basket, then, feeling embarrassed, took a step back. Who took lunch to their child's teacher? "Chicken salad sandwich, a banana and a whoopie pie." She took another step back. "I made the whoopie pies last night."

"Whoopie pie?" He peeked beneath the cloth napkin that covered the basket. "I do love a homemade whoopie pie. My mother used to make a great one. She passed a few years ago."

"I'm sorry," Abigail said softly. Mention of his mother immediately made her think of her own. She couldn't imagine losing her. She knew it would happen someday, in God's good time, but not when Abigail was still so young. Even with her mother's memory issues and strange behavior, Abigail still learned from her every day. June King still had plenty to offer not just to her daughter, but to her husband, grandson and community.

"My mother always said I had a sweet tooth." Ethan grimaced. "I've had whoopie pies store-bought, but they're just not the same as made from scratch."

"Well, I hope you enjoy it. The whoopie pie. The lunch. I'll be back to walk Jamie home after school."

He held up the basket. "Thank you. I'll return the basket."

She nodded, walking backward. "No hurry." She pressed her lips together and then said, "I guess I'll be seeing you every day this week. Twice a day." Then, feeling more like one of the teen girls in the coatroom than a widowed mother, she turned and hurried out of the schoolroom. That afternoon, she promised herself, she'd wait for her son at the end of the driveway. She wouldn't come inside. That way she wouldn't have to talk to Ethan again. In fact, if her son would behave himself, she'd never have to speak to him again.

Ethan approached four girls seated together at their desks near the rear of the classroom. The students were talking quietly, but there was clearly a disagreement going on. The third and fourth graders were working together on identifying all of the states on a US map. It was their second day on the project. The previous day, the girls had done pretty well on the East and West Coast, but they had struggled in the Midwest.

"Questions?" Ethan asked, leaning over to address ten-year-old Liz Fisher who had been the self-appointed leader of the group since school had begun in September.

Because he was trying to teach so many students of different ages and abilities, Ethan had found it helpful to divide them by approximate grades and then by boys and girls. There were some activities where girls and boys worked together, but often there was more hair pulling and squealing than concentration on lessons, so he didn't do it often. Usually this group of girls, as with most of the girls in the school, were self-sufficient once given an assignment. That gave him more time to work with the boys or his three eighth-grade boys who wouldn't likely be returning to school the following September. Most Amish families took their children out at that age. The girls would work in the houses and gardens with their mothers and boys on their farms with their fathers. The boys sometimes even got jobs in construction. Ethan had been fortunate enough that his father had encouraged him to complete high school, which enabled him to be a schoolteacher.

"Hannah says that's New Mexico," Liz said in *Deitsch*, pointing at the outline of New Mexico.

"English, please," Ethan told her. His policy was to always speak English, unless a child didn't understand something and then he would switch to Pennsylvania *Deitsch*. It was his belief, and the school board's, that one of his duties as the schoolmaster was to be sure all of the students spoke English well enough to function in the Englishers' world.

Liz switched to English. "I told her and told her it was Arizona, but she won't let me write it in." She pointed at the paper on Hannah Gruber's desk. While Liz was currently leader of the four of them, Hannah had been making a move for the position for weeks.

"What do you think, Mary?" Ethan asked, turning his attention to the younger student. Mary Kutz, a nine-year-old, was Hannah's cousin.

Mary nibbled on her lower lip and whispered something. The child was painfully shy.

"What was that?" Ethan asked. His inclination was to lean closer to her, but he was working hard to encourage Mary Kutz to speak up. She was an excellent student; he'd seriously considered moving her up at Christmas to the fifth- and sixth-year group, but he was worried she would wilt amid that set of bossy girls. What Mary needed more was not to be promoted to a higher grade, but to find a healthy dose of confidence.

Ethan waited for Mary to repeat what she'd said.

"New Mexico," she murmured with a slight lisp. She

pointed to the correct state. "Arizona." She indicated that state, then rattled off three more, touching with her finger each state that was yet to be identified. "Utah, Colorado, Kansas," she said.

He smiled at her. "Excellent!" He stood to his full height. "So Hannah is correct, Liz." He slid the piece of paper and a pencil to Mary. "Why don't you label them?"

The timid girl took the pencil and immediately began to neatly print the names of the states in the proper places.

Ethan looked to Hannah's little sister Lettice who sat quietly in her seat, hands folded, watching Mary. Lettice was one of his two students who had Down's Syndrome. While families often chose not to send children with disabilities to school, Ethan thought the Grubers had made a wise choice in allowing Lettice and her twin brother, Esau, to begin the previous September. He often put Lettice with the younger girls. She'd already learned to write her name and could count to fifty. But she was more comfortable being with her big sister, so Ethan allowed her to divide her day between the two groups. He didn't know how much geography and science she was learning, but she seemed content. And she never misbehaved, which was more than he could say for some of his students.

"Ethan?"

He felt a tug on his sleeve and looked over his shoulder to see his stepbrother Jesse standing beside him. Jesse was an average student, but a good kid. "Jamie," Jesse said under his breath.

Ethan exhaled, trying to keep his patience intact, said

something encouraging to the girls and then turned to his brother. "What is it?"

"I know we're not supposed to tattle, but…" He nervously tugged at a forelock of his hair.

"Yes?"

"He won't leave us alone. We're trying to take that division quiz you gave us, but he keeps hitting us with… stuff."

Ethan arched his eyebrow. "Stuff?"

"Spitballs," Jesse whispered, looking down. "He got me right here." He pointed to his cheek. There was a distinct red mark.

Ethan glanced at Jamie who appeared to be concentrating on his reader. He looked back at his brother. "Go back to your seat. Finish your quiz." He gave Jesse's shoulder a squeeze and then crossed the room to where Jamie sat alone at a desk. Earlier in the day he'd been with the first and second graders, but he'd scribbled all over his neighbor's book and then tried to lie his way out of it.

Jamie spotted Ethan coming toward him and immediately tucked something into the back of his pants. The boy picked up his pencil and stared at the worksheet in front of him intently.

"Spitballs again?" Ethan asked him quietly.

Jamie didn't respond, which Ethan supposed was a step in the right direction. At least he hadn't flat-out lied to him this time.

Ethan stood over the boy's desk, looking down at the worksheet. Jamie was supposed to have read the next chapter in his reading book and then answered the questions. Had he been able to behave himself, he could have done the assignment with a partner. Instead, he was doing it alone.

Jamie hadn't filled in a single answer. And the answers weren't that difficult. Their reader was a simple one from the 1940s that he'd found six copies of at Spence's Bazaar. The story Jamie was supposed to have read was one about a boy and a dog going fishing. All Jamie had to do was answer questions like what color the dog was and what he had done earlier in the day.

"You haven't answered a single question," Ethan said, pointing at the blank page. The corner of the paper was conspicuously missing.

Jamie said nothing.

"Did you read the story?" Ethan asked. Technically, Jamie was a third grader. The story was written on a first-grade level. By Ethan's calculation, the boy should have been done with the assignment half an hour ago.

Jamie stared at the paper on his desk. He hadn't even written his name on it.

Ethan took a deep breath. "Okay." He placed his finger beside the first question. "What was the dog's name in the story?"

Jamie was quiet.

"What was its name?" Ethan repeated. "Easy question."

"I don't remember," the boy answered softly.

"Okay…" Ethan opened the book to the first page of the story. "Right here, second line." He pointed at the word. Waited.

Jamie lowered his head. "I don't know," he said under his breath.

"So read it out loud." Ethan tapped on the word.

"*F…*" The boy made the sound of the first letter. "*F…*" he repeated. He squirmed in his seat. "Fred!" he declared.

Ethan frowned. "Look again. Sound it out. *F… I…*"

"Fireman?" Jamie asked.

"Now you're just guessing." Ethan looked down at the boy. "Can you see that word?" he asked, wondering if the boy needed glasses. "What are the letters?"

Jamie groaned and ran his finger under the word. "*F... I... Um... D.*" He exhaled loudly. *"O?"*

"*O*, that's right. Which spells what?" Ethan asked when the boy was quiet again.

Jamie pressed his lips together staring at the page.

"Fido," Ethan said. Then he squatted down, looked into Jamie's eyes and knew at once what was happening. "You can't read, can you?" he asked softly.

Still Jamie didn't speak.

How had Ethan missed this? He thought back to the times he'd believed Jamie was misbehaving for not being attentive to reading assignments. He'd attributed his lack of progress to mischievousness, his blank assignment papers as just more willful disobedience.

Feeling guilty that he hadn't been more attentive to the child, hadn't recognized it sooner, Ethan stood and squeezed Jamie's shoulder. "We'll get back to this tomorrow. Why don't you gather the erasers and pick a buddy to go outside with you and clean them?"

Jamie popped out of his chair, needing no further encouragement.

Ethan watched him go. They had only another twenty minutes until school was over. The erasers would keep Jamie busy until it was time to gather his things. And then Abigail would be there to pick up her son.

And Ethan and Abigail were going to have to have a talk.

Chapter Four

Abigail stood off to the side of the driveway as children left on push scooters in groups of three or four. They had all hooked their lunch bags, baskets or pails on the handlebars and wore fluorescent orange vests so that motorists could spot them on the country road more easily. She could see that most of the students *did* have scooters, but not all of them. Some of the children left on foot by the road while others took a path through the woods behind the schoolhouse.

As she waited for Jamie to come out, she thought about whether or not she should buy him a scooter, rather than holding it over his head as a reward for better behavior. It wasn't as if she didn't have money to buy one. Unlike many widows, her husband had left her with a tidy bank account, and after the sale of their house and one-hundred-acre farm, she had more money than she had the need for. But her father had cautioned her about spending too much on Jamie. He thought it would spoil him, making him feel as if he was in some way better than other children, isolating him from his community. Her father had even criticized her for making her son new clothing and buying him new boots. She'd reminded him that he was an only child and that she had no hand-me-downs to give Jamie, but he'd stubbornly maintained that a boy shouldn't look so fancy.

One by one, the students left the schoolyard and soon it was empty. But Jamie didn't appear. Abigail had wanted to wait for him outside so she wouldn't have to encounter Ethan again. She'd made her apology to him. She saw no need to speak with him again. But she supposed she was going to have to go into the school to retrieve her son. She hoped he wasn't in trouble again. With a sigh, she walked along the oyster shell driveway, up the steps and pushed open the door to the cloakroom—almost running right into Ethan.

"Oh!" she exclaimed, backing down the steps. "I didn't— I was waiting for Jamie. He hadn't—"

"Here I am," Jamie piped up from behind the schoolmaster.

She stood in the grass looking up, feeling flustered and she didn't know why.

Ethan held her basket in his hand. He didn't look happy, but he didn't seem angry either, so maybe her son wasn't in trouble. "Jamie was helping me put some books away," he said.

"Was he?" Abigail asked, relieved his behavior wasn't the issue.

"Ya." Ethan stood on the top step and let Jamie go by him, then locked the door with a key. "We thought we'd walk home together." He shrugged, coming down the steps. "Since we're going the same way. Right, Jamie?"

Abigail looked at Jamie, finding it hard to believe her son had agreed to walk home with his schoolteacher, considering how he felt about him. Jamie hadn't come right out and said he disliked Ethan, probably because he knew better than to say such a thing. But it was clear the schoolmaster was not her boy's favorite person in Hickory Grove.

"That okay with you?" Ethan asked Abigail, slipping the key ring into his pocket. "Your place is on the way to mine if I go by way of the road."

"You…you didn't bring your buggy?" she asked, feeling silly the moment the words came out of her mouth. Of course he hadn't driven his buggy this morning. If he had, he'd be taking it home. And she'd certainly have seen his horse tied up at the hitching post. A horse that color couldn't be missed. She groaned inwardly, wondering what on earth had gotten into her. She was usually so levelheaded. Never flighty.

"I walked. Thought I'd enjoy the nice weather," Ethan said, not seeming to think her question had been silly. "I like walking when the weather is decent. On the walk here in the morning, I get my lesson plans straight in my head. On the walk home, I… I think Englishers use the word *decompress*." He met her gaze, still solemn but not annoyed.

She wondered what made him such a sober man. Was it his job as a schoolmaster? She thought not. But there was definitely a sadness in his eyes. She wondered if his marriage was an unhappy one and that thought saddened her. She and her husband, Egan, had married for love. Her parents, as well. But not all Amish couples had that luxury. Sometimes marriages were arranged by parents, sometimes they were made for financial reasons and sometimes women like her, *often* women like her, single with children, married a man suitable to be a husband and father. Their faith believed in the responsibility of all men and women to be married; romance was only a secondary consideration.

"I think about whatever has gone on that day and then I try to let it go," Ethan continued. "Helps me look at things fresh the next day."

She nodded, imagining taking that time to *decompress*, as he called it, helped him to be a better husband, a better father. If he had children. She didn't know if he did. She'd not been in the community long enough to have knowledge of such details of her neighbors yet. It was on the tip of her tongue to ask, but for some reason, she didn't feel like she should. It somehow seemed too...*personal* to be asking such a question of her son's teacher.

Instead, she turned her attention to Jamie as the three of them set out for home. "What did you do in school today?"

"Um." Jamie held up his lunch pail for her to take. "We played softball during recess. I got out two times. But I made a good catch at third base," he added, seeming pleased with himself.

"Sounds like you had fun." Abigail reached out to take his lunch pail, then pulled her hand back. "Carry it yourself." She looked back at Ethan. "I can take my basket."

"I'll carry it as far as your place. It was good, the lunch. And the whoopie pie?" Ethan made a sound that was very near to delight, which took her by surprise. "Delicious. *Danke.*"

She couldn't help but smile. So maybe he wasn't always such a sour man. "I'm glad you liked it." She almost blurted that her husband, Egan, had loved her whoopie pies, too, but she caught herself before she said it. She didn't speak often about Egan, and never to strangers. At first, she was afraid it was because she hadn't cared enough for him. It had been her mother who had pointed out that sometimes the deepest feelings are the ones that are the hardest to share.

"Your timing was perfect," Ethan continued. "The John Yoder twins both forgot their lunches. So they shared my bologna sandwich and potato chips and I had your chicken salad. I think I got the better deal for once. I like the little peppers in it. What were they?"

"Pimento," she said. "And I always add a pinch of cayenne pepper."

"Take it, *Mam*." Jamie stubbornly bumped her hand with his pail. "Please?" He drew out the word.

"Carry it yourself," she said a little sternly. "You're old enough to carry your own lunch, to and from school."

"But you used to always carry it for me when we lived in Wisconsin."

Jamie's whining tone embarrassed her and she took a breath before she responded. "But now you're older and you can do it yourself." She glanced over her shoulder at Ethan again. The grassy patch that ran along the side of the road was wide enough for two to walk side by side, but not three so he had taken up the rear. She looked forward again. "What else did you do in school, *sohn*?"

"Um… At lunch we watched a bunch of ants eat part of the crust of Jesse's bologna sandwich. They took away little tiny pieces. To their house, Jesse told us. They leave something behind so they know their way back. Fair… Fair somethings."

"Pheromones," Ethan put in. Then to Abigail he explained, "We've been talking about insects in our sixth-grade class. My brother Jesse is in that group."

She nodded. She didn't know that ants left a trail for themselves, but she had always wondered how they could wander so far from their anthills and still find their way home. She was impressed that Ethan knew such a fact and that he had shared it with his students. "That must have been interesting about the ants," she said to her son. "But I meant in school. What did you do *in class* today?"

"I don't know." He kicked at a tuft of dandelions and the fuzzy seeds blew away in the breeze. "Nothing."

"*Nothing?* I think if I asked your teacher, he might say you'd done *something* in school all day."

Neither her son nor Ethan responded, and Abigail let the subject drop. Instead, she walked in silence, enjoying the warm sunshine and the scent of freshly turned soil in the field they walked beside. Jamie slowly made his way forward until he was in front of her and the three of them walked single file.

A buggy approached them from behind and Ethan waved. They slowed down. Abigail didn't know the couple, but she smiled. The passenger door slid open and a woman who looked to be in her fifties smiled and nodded her head in greeting.

"New neighbor, Abigail Stolz, daughter of June and Daniel King. Just moved here from Wisconsin. And my student Jamie—Abigail's son," Ethan introduced. He pointed to the buggy. "Hannah and Albert Hartman."

"Good to have you here, Abigail," the woman called. "We need young families. Too many folks moving away. Will we see you at the Brubachers' Saturday?"

Abigail looked over her shoulder at Ethan questioningly.

"I'm sure you will," Ethan called to the older woman

who Abigail took an immediate liking to. Hannah had a sparkle in her eyes that seemed mischievous and kind at the same time.

"I'll let her know all about it," Ethan promised.

"See you there!" Hannah waved enthusiastically and the buggy picked up its pace and pulled away.

"They live over in Seven Poplars," Ethan said when they had gone by. "North of here." He pointed in the general direction. "Interesting man, Albert. He's a veterinarian. Takes care of most Amish families' livestock in the whole county."

"An Amish veterinarian?" Abigail asked in surprise, looking back at him.

"They're pretty amazing, the both of them." Ethan caught up to her and walked beside her. "Second marriage for Hannah," he explained. "Hannah's husband died, leaving her with six girls to raise. She stayed single for years while she raised her girls. Taught school over at Seven Poplars. Albert was a bachelor. He was Mennonite but became Amish so he could marry Hannah. Funny thing is, Hannah was Mennonite, too, before she married her first husband."

"And their bishop allows him to continue to be a veterinarian?" she asked in wonder.

"Sure does. With restrictions, of course." Ethan slid his hand into his pocket as he walked beside her. "No work on Sundays. Not even for his Amish clients. He has someone on call for him on Sundays. But he's allowed to drive his work truck because he just does large animals—cows, sheep, horses and such." He pointed at her. "Oh, and alpacas."

Abigail laughed. "What's an alpaca?"

"Like a llama. Albert has a bunch of them."

She shook her head with a chuckle. It certainly didn't sound very Amish. "Why does he have alpacas?"

"Apparently their wool is worth something. I don't know that he makes much profit off it, but he likes them. Likes the oddity of them, I think."

She nodded, thinking she might like to see these alpacas. And she imagined Jamie would, too.

"Anyway, what Hannah was talking about," Ethan went on, "is a barn raising going on Saturday. Everyone in the area is invited. It's for the Brubachers. They live over toward Marydel, which is west of here. The family lost their main barn in the fall to a lightning strike. The whole thing went up so fast, Abner barely had time to get his horses and cows out. You and your parents and Jamie should come. Good way to meet more folks."

"I haven't been to a barn raising in years," Abigail mused aloud as they made a right-hand turn onto her road. "I bet my *dat* and *mam* would enjoy it." She was learning that it was good for her mother to get out with people. Her mother's head seemed clearer when she didn't spend so much time alone with just their small family.

He shrugged. "Like I said, everyone is welcome. The more folks there, the faster the barn will go up. There will be a big dinner of course, and it looks like we're going to have a good day for it. Sunny and seventy degrees."

Jamie turned around to face his mother. "Can I run ahead?"

Abigail hesitated.

"Please?" Her son bounced on the balls of his feet, his lunch pail banging against his leg. He was obviously a bundle of energy after sitting at his desk all day.

"Fine," she agreed.

The boy took off.

"But you better stay away from Karl's cows!" she hollered after him. Then she sighed. "Boys." She glanced at Ethan. "I suppose you think I should have made him walk beside me all the way home." Her tone suddenly grew prickly. She was enjoying the walk home with Ethan, but that didn't mean she hadn't forgotten the animosity between them. "To *discipline* him."

"I see no trouble letting him run ahead. You'll be able to see him if he climbs Karl's fence." Ethan glanced at her and then ahead again. "I wanted to talk to you alone anyway."

She looked at him and back at the grassy path trampled by others who took the same route to and from school. "What's he done now?" She said it almost as an exhalation. Her day had been a long one already.

She and her father had had words when she had come home from dropping Jamie off at school. She'd arrived to find her mother trying to make bread using a cup of warm vinegar instead of water to dissolve the yeast. Her father had made light of the incident, saying her mother had just "forgotten." Abigail had argued that a woman seventy years old, who had been making bread since she was ten, did not *forget* how to make it. She felt there was more going on with her mother than forgetfulness but no matter what happened, her father insisted there was nothing wrong. He usually countered any argument with Abigail on the subject by recalling an incident where he'd forgotten to pick up an item on the grocery list or left a feed bin open for the chickens to get into. And she always responded with the fact that it wasn't the same, but her father was an obstinate man, especially when it came to the subject of his wife.

Abigail didn't look at Ethan. She just put one foot in front of another. This was probably something trivial again. Obviously the schoolmaster didn't like her son and he was going to take every opportunity he could to pick on the boy.

"I wanted to talk to you about—" Ethan went quiet for a moment and then blurted, "Abigail, I don't think Jamie can read."

She halted and turned to him. *"What?"* she demanded with a mixture of indignation and disbelief.

Ethan met her gaze. He didn't seem angry, only concerned. "I don't think he can read. No," he corrected himself. "I'm sure of it."

"That's ridiculous. I've heard him read," she argued, settling her hands on her hips.

"You've heard him read what?"

"Um…" She thought for a moment. It wasn't as if students brought their reading books home and read aloud to their parents at night. Reading was for school. And understanding that children, no matter their age, had chores to do when they got home, Ethan didn't often give homework. "I don't know. A sign in the grocery store? On…on a feed bag."

Ethan shook his head no. "That doesn't mean he's reading. He's a smart boy. I think he's guessing."

She dropped one hand from her hip, her annoyance with him rising by the second. "What do you mean?"

"He knows the sounds of most of his letters, but he's using context clues to guess the word. The pictures. Or the item. Sure, he can read a sign that says apples because he can see the apples in the bin. A bag of chicken feed?" He lifted his hand and let it fall. "A chicken on the bag."

Abigail walked. They had almost reached her father's driveway. She could see that Jamie was nearly to the house. "That's ridiculous," she repeated again. "Jamie is... He's bright. Mischievous, but...bright. And he's good with math. He adds and subtracts well. Multiplies."

Ethan caught up to her and walked beside her again. "You're right. Jamie is bright. And he's also good with math in his head. But I've been a teacher here for years now and I know a student who can't read when I see one."

She reached the driveway and turned to face the schoolteacher, feeling defensive. "Jamie started school when he was six, right on time," she sputtered. "His teacher back home never told me he couldn't read."

"Was he getting into trouble at his old school?"

She didn't answer.

"That's often an indication of a problem with learning. Students who aren't learning at the same pace as other students their age, slower *or* faster, act out from boredom. Or sometimes frustration."

"I have to get home." Abigail took her basket out of his hand, being none too gentle.

"Me, too." He walked past the driveway, then turned back to her. "It would be easy enough for you to see for yourself. Test him."

She didn't know what to say, maybe because the thought crossed her mind that possibly Jamie couldn't read as well as he should have been able to. She immediately thought of a couple of instances over the last year when he'd misread something. But she'd just chalked it up to all the changes in his life. The idea that a nine-year-old boy couldn't read, *her* nine-year-old, was absurd.

"Test him," Ethan repeated, heading down the road. "Then we'll talk."

That evening, after the supper dishes had been cleared away, the family had settled in the living room for an hour before bed. Abigail was still fuming about what Ethan had told her. Of course Jamie could read. Maybe he just didn't want to read for Ethan. Maybe the subject in his reading book was boring. There had to be a dozen explanations.

But what if Ethan was right? That thought had been creeping into her head since she'd discussed it with him earlier in the day.

Abigail glanced up from the list she was making for their trip to Byler's store the next day. They needed groceries, including several items to make the macaroni salad her mother wanted to take to the barn raising on Saturday. It turned out that her father had already heard about the community event when he was at the harness shop that morning—the harness shop owned by Ethan's father. At supper, her father had announced that he told Benjamin Miller he would help and that they would all be going to the barn raising in Marydel. He'd been assigned to a work crew right on the spot.

Abigail tapped her pencil on the pad of paper on her lap. Her mother was sound asleep in an old recliner that had been left in the house by the previous owner. Her father and Jamie were playing a game of checkers.

"And that's your last one," her father announced,

skipping over Jamie's black checker with his red one. "I won."

Jamie frowned, crossing his arms over his chest. "You never let me win."

"No, I do not. But if you listen to what I tell you, you'll be beating me on your own in no time," his grandfather said, beginning to reset the board for the next time they would play.

Abigail watched her son for a moment and then called his name.

Jamie looked over as he got out of his chair. *"Ya?"*

She waved him over with the pencil in her hand. "Come here for a second." As he crossed the cozy living room, she turned the pad of paper around so that she could point out one of the words she'd printed neatly on the page. "What does that say?" she asked, tapping beside the word *pears.*

Jamie looked down and then up at his mother, suddenly seeming uncomfortable.

"That's…that's your shopping list," he said.

"Ya," she agreed. "And I want you to tell me what that word is on my list."

"I'm tired," he whined. "I want to go to bed."

"You can go in just a second." A feeling of dread was growing stronger inside her with every second. What if Ethan had been right? What if her son couldn't read? "Read the word to me, Jamie," she said, the tone of her voice telling him she wouldn't tolerate disobedience.

He groaned loudly. *"P…p…"* he repeated the sound. "Potatoes!" he exclaimed.

She didn't know what to say. She tapped the next word on the list: *crackers.*

Jamie stared at it. *"K… k…"* He looked up at her.

"I don't know. Your writing is messy." He wiped at his eyes that had suddenly turned teary. "May I go to bed? I'm tired."

She hesitated, then rose from her chair and kissed the top of his head. "You may."

"What was that all about?" Abigail's father asked as Jamie hurried out of the room.

"I'll tell you later," she whispered. Then she carried the pad of paper into the dark kitchen, not sure what she was more upset about at that moment. Was it that Jamie couldn't read, or that she was going to have to apologize to Ethan Miller again?

Chapter Five

By eight on Saturday morning, the sound of hammers and saws echoed across the Brubacher farm. The day was bright, the grass still damp with dew and the air filled with the scent of spring blossoming around them. It was a good day, and Abigail was grateful to God for the gentle weather.

Next to the family's farmhouse, women and girls set up tables in the yard, while boys took charge of arriving horses and buggies. At the construction site in the barnyard, eight men were already raising the frame of the first wall on the new barn. According to Abigail's father, because the block foundation was in place and the poured cement floor laid, they would have four walls and a roof by sunset.

Friends and neighbors were coming from every direction, on foot, in wagons piled high with lumber, in buggies, and on push scooters. Abigail and a young woman she'd met that morning, Phoebe, walked among the men offering mugs of steaming coffee and breakfast sandwiches wrapped in aluminum foil to keep them hot.

"Sausage, egg and cheese on an English muffin or

bacon, egg and cheese?" Phoebe asked a handsome young man who looked to be in his early to midtwenties.

Phoebe had introduced herself the moment Abigail and her family had arrived and had quickly steered each of them in a different direction. She'd sent Abigail's father to speak with Abner Brubacher who was overseeing the barn raising. She'd taken Abigail's mother to join a group of older women at a picnic table where they were wrapping silverware in paper napkins for the noonday meal. And to Jamie's delight, Phoebe had waved Ethan's brother Jesse over. The two boys had run off with talk of fetching nails for the men, and Abigail hadn't seen her son since.

"Which ones did you make?" the man asked Phoebe, pointing at the basket of hot sandwiches her new friend was carrying. The way he was grinning, Abigail suspected that he was smitten with Phoebe.

"None of them," Phoebe answered, smiling back at him. "Bacon or sausage, choose quick, or I'll be choosing for you."

Phoebe's brash statement, combined with obvious flirting, confused Abigail. She knew that for an Old Order community Hickory Grove was relatively relaxed, but the way these two were looking at each other was certainly not something she witnessed often. It embarrassed her and tickled her at the same time. And made her miss her husband.

"Abigail." Phoebe turned to her. "This is Joshua Miller. My husband," she added, looking back at him.

Abigail smiled. He was her husband. That made sense, though they were still rather flirty with each other.

"And my husband is getting bacon, egg and cheese because we have more of those left," Phoebe went on as she took a foil-wrapped sandwich from her basket and offered it to him. "This is my new friend, Abigail. She just moved here from northern Wisconsin. Her parents are June and Daniel King. I know you've met Daniel at the harness shop. They live right down the road from us."

Joshua propped his hammer against the foundation and accepted the sandwich.

"Coffee?" Phoebe asked.

"Sure. Thanks."

"There certainly are a lot of Millers here." Abigail only said it to make conversation. There had been a lot of Amish Millers in Wisconsin, too. "My son's teacher is a Miller, too."

Joshua took a sip of the coffee he'd taken off the tray, his gaze moving from his wife to Abigail. "That would be my big brother, Ethan."

"Oh… I… I didn't know." Abigail looked down at the tray in her hands not understanding why this information surprised her or why she cared. Ethan had already told her he would be there. In fact, she'd spotted him when her family arrived. He was one of the men now securing the first wall of the barn.

"My other brothers are here, too. Well, Jacob, Will and Jesse. Our brother Levi is living in Lancaster, apprenticing as a buggy maker." He cut his eyes at his wife. "At least that's the story he's giving us. We all have a notion he's there because the courting pond is larger. Levi has a bit of a reputation for being a ladies' man."

Phoebe frowned, but only half-heartedly. "You shouldn't say such things, Joshua." She looked to Abigail. "He means a ladies' man in an Amish kind of way."

She shook her head. "Not in the way Englishers mean it. Levi's a good man, faithful and good-hearted." She shrugged. "He just likes to flirt."

"He'd be flirting with you, Abigail, if he was here. I guarantee you that. You being single and all." Joshua set down his coffee and began to unwrap his breakfast sandwich. "He keeps trying to give Ethan tips on how to get a girl's attention. He's been pushing hard lately. Every time we see Levi, he's trying to introduce Ethan to a girl he thinks might be suitable."

Abigail knit her brows. "Wait, Ethan is— I thought he was married."

Phoebe shook her head no, ever so slightly.

Abigail wouldn't have been any more surprised than if Joshua had just said that the next load of wood coming in from the sawmill would be on the back of an elephant. "But he has a beard," she argued. "Married men have beards. Single men don't."

Phoebe's face softened. "Widowed." She looked to her husband. "What? Going on six years now?" Her tone was soft and kind.

Joshua held his sandwich but didn't take a bite. "About that." He glanced at Abigail. "His wife, Mary, had epilepsy. She had a seizure and passed away."

"She's with the Lord now," Phoebe said gently.

Abigail bowed her head. "I… I assumed that because he had the beard," she stammered, "that he…" She stopped and started again. "Where I come from, a clean-shaven man is unmarried, a married man has a beard."

"It's that way here, too." Joshua took a bite of his sandwich. "But when you get to widowers, the rules aren't so black-and-white. Our friend Eli is widowed.

He had a beard for some time after his wife passed, but now he's shaved it. He said that, for him, it was part of the mourning process. I can't imagine what it must be like to lose your wife or your husband." He looked at Phoebe. "If I lost my Phoebe—" His voice caught in his throat and Phoebe reached out with one hand and rubbed his shoulder.

"I'm not going anywhere, silly," Phoebe murmured to him. Then she looked at Abigail and said, "And I'm sorry about your husband."

"It's been three years," Abigail answered.

"Doesn't matter." Phoebe smiled. "I'm still sorry for you and for your son."

Nodding, Abigail pressed her lips together looking away from them. Joshua reminded her a little of her father. Amish men didn't always talk so freely about such things. She had liked Joshua the moment she met him, but she liked him even more now.

Her thoughts darted from one place to the next. Joshua's brother was Ethan. Ethan who was *not* married. She didn't know why but the idea made her feel completely off balance. Because of the way he had handled Jamie, obviously she didn't care for him. But a part of her suddenly felt almost attracted to him. Which fascinated her and dismayed her at the same time.

"Mam!" Jamie's voice drew her attention.

She turned to see him and Jesse and a boy she didn't know running toward them. "Jesse's *mam* said you had sandwiches," Jamie huffed, out of breath from running. "We're hungry."

Abigail had fed Jamie a nice breakfast of buckwheat hotcakes with honey from Fifer's orchard, scrapple and stewed apples with cinnamon before they came that morning, but his appetite seemed endless these days. Her mother said it was because he was growing. "Do we have enough or are these just for the men working?" she asked Phoebe.

Phoebe gave a wave of dismissal. She was such an attractive woman with light brown hair and blue eyes. She had a son, too: John, who was younger than Jamie. "We have plenty of sandwiches. And Claudia—you met her earlier. This is her new barn. She's got more eggs and meat frying on her cookstove."

"Are you boys helping with the building?" Abigail asked as she nodded, indicating Jamie could take a sandwich from the basket Phoebe offered.

"Ne." Joshua finished off the last bites of his sandwich and handed his wife the crumpled foil. "These rascals would be more in the way than they're worth. Back to the house with the three of you," he ordered, retrieving his coffee mug from the tailgate of the wagon where he'd set it down. "Tend to the horses and do whatever the women ask."

"Good behavior," Abigail warned her son as the three boys took off.

"Joshua!" a man called from the far end of the first wall frame. "We need you on this beam."

"Guess I better get back to work." Joshua nodded to the women and, taking his coffee with him, strode toward the place where the men had begun construction of another wall on the ground.

"You're going to have to put the coffee down," the man who called to Joshua hollered.

Abigail looked up to see a man who looked identical to Joshua speaking to him and she glanced at Phoebe. "Your husband is a twin." It wasn't a question. Most large Amish families had at least one set of twins. Abigail had known a family in her old church district that had *three* sets of twins.

"That would be Jacob. He's unmarried, too." Phoebe started walking and Abigail went with her. "Very sweet. Good-natured. Loves animals. He'd make a good husband, too."

The look on Phoebe's face made Abigail chuckle. "Who said I was looking for a husband?"

"Actually your mother. She told all of us." She wrinkled her nose. "But I think she has her heart set on Ethan. Who would also make a good husband. I'm not saying he wouldn't. He's just a little more…*reserved* is maybe the right word…than Benjamin's other sons."

Abigail barely heard what Phoebe had said about Ethan. She knew she was blushing. She could feel the heat rising from her neck upward. She imagined her face had to be bright red. "I can't believe my mother would—" She was so embarrassed that she didn't know what to say.

"Oh, Abigail, don't be upset." Phoebe stopped and touched Abigail's arm. "You know women. We talk. It's only natural. Mothers want husbands for their girls. Girls want husbands, families. It's one of our favorite things to natter about when the men aren't around. She meant no harm."

Abigail stared at the ground. "I know I'll marry again. That I should. I only wish my mother wouldn't—" She exhaled. "It's awkward that she would bring up Ethan. He and I, we haven't—" She searched for the right thing to say without being critical of Phoebe's brother-in-law. "There's been a bit of trouble at school with my Jamie. Ethan and I had words. I suspect I'm not exactly his favorite person right now."

"*Ne?* Then why's he waving to you?" She pointed.

Abigail looked up to see Ethan, not twenty yards away. He had just lowered an armful of timber to the ground. He was wearing a straw hat like the other men, but he'd rolled up his sleeves to bare his arms. The thought went through her head that he was awfully muscular for a schoolteacher. Then she was embarrassed all over again.

"Good morning, Abigail," Ethan called to her. "You have a minute?"

Before Abigail could respond, Phoebe took the tray that had only two coffee mugs on it from her. "Go on." Then she whispered, "He doesn't seem upset with you to me."

Abigail offered a quick smile at Ethan and walked toward him. The dew was beginning to dry from the grass and the sweet smell of fresh-cut lumber filled the air. The sound of hammers hitting nails rang out and somehow the familiarity of it all, even though she was now so far from home, comforted her. It reminded her of the goodness in God's world. "I'm helping with the breakfast," she said as she approached him.

"I've got another load to haul." He pointed to the lumber in the grass. "Just take a second." When she was close enough that no one else could hear them, he said, "Listen, Abigail… I feel like I owe you an apology."

She looked up at him. Into his brown eyes. For the first time, she noticed his blond hair was a little long. Which made sense because he was obviously in his thirties; a man in his thirties usually had a wife to cut his hair. But he was widowed. And his mother was dead, too. She wondered who did it for him. His father's new wife?

"An apology? What for?" she asked. "I was the one who was rude to you."

He shook his head. "I shouldn't have blurted it out that way. About Jamie. His inability to read."

"But you were right," she told him, holding his gaze. "And I was wrong. I was wrong to snap at you the way I did, and I was wrong not to trust you as his teacher."

He shook his head. "Doesn't matter that I'm his teacher. It was unkind of me to tell you that way. It was just that I was…frustrated."

"I know how trying Jamie can be." She gave a chuckle, feeling herself relax. "Believe me. I of all people know."

He smiled at her. "So you tested him?"

She nodded, looking down at her sneakers damp from the earlier morning dew. She'd worn her favorite everyday dress today, blue, bright like a midsummer sky in Wisconsin. For some reason she was glad she had. She looked up at him again. "I was making a grocery list and I asked him to read it to me. No…" She searched for the phrase he'd use. "No *context clues*," she said. "He thought the word *pears* was the word *potatoes*." To her chagrin, emotion had suddenly clogged her voice. What if Jamie couldn't learn to read? Even in their slower-paced world, Amish men and women needed to know how to read. They needed to be able to read because they still lived in the Englisher's world. They had to use Englisher grocery stores, banks, doctors' offices.

"Hey, hey," Ethan said gently, taking a step toward her. He didn't touch her of course. That wouldn't have been appropriate. But the tone of his voice was comforting. Almost like a hug. "It's going to be okay. I promise you."

"Ethan!" someone called. "We need a hand here! Something's not quite square. Jacob says it Joshua's fault. Joshua says it's Jacob's," he finished good-naturedly.

Ethan glanced in the direction of a group of men. "Coming!" He looked back at her. "I have to go but—"

"*Ne*, it's fine." She took a step back, suddenly feeling self-conscious. The thought went through her mind: *He's not married. He's widowed like me. He understands what it's like to be alone.* "I have to get back to help with the…the coffee and breakfast sandwiches."

He walked away, calling over his shoulder, "Let's talk when we break for dinner." He pointed. "I'll come find you. And don't worry. Jamie is going to be fine. I promise."

Oddly enough, there was something in his voice that made Abigail think he was right. Her boy really was going to be fine.

Carrying his plate heaped with sandwiches, salads and assorted casseroles, Ethan walked around the side of the house in search of Abigail. The grass here was nearly knee-high in places, and the previous year's dried up Queen Anne's lace and black-eyed Susans lingered, adding their brown and gold stalks to the green carpet sprouting up all around. He'd spotted Jamie's mother walking this way a moment ago. He couldn't miss her in that blue dress that made her eyes seem even bluer.

"There you are," he called, spotting her as she walked away from a group of his students sitting under a blossoming peach tree. He was pleased to see that Jamie was among the boys. He'd specifically asked Jesse to be sure to include Jamie in the day's activities, reminding his little brother what it had been like when they'd moved here to Delaware and he hadn't known anyone.

"Ethan." She smiled at him and he was relieved to see that even though they had gotten off to a bad start, maybe she wasn't the sort to hold a grudge.

He walked up to her. The voices of men and women talking and laughing drifted from the backyard where tables were set up to eat. They'd had such a great turn-out, though, that there weren't nearly enough seats for the men who would eat at the first sitting.

Ordinarily, at this type of event, the men ate first, then once they had returned to work, the women and children ate. Due to the limited seating, one of the women had made the decision that the elders and those with physical issues would take seats at the tables. The younger men and teenaged boys, and those children who couldn't wait another moment to eat had found steps or a shady place under a tree to enjoy their meals.

"I thought maybe we could talk while we eat," Ethan told Abigail.

"Oh, I don't know. I should…" She glanced over her shoulder. "I should probably go back to help serve. I was just checking on Jamie. I was going to eat later. With the other women. Once the men go back to work," she explained, working her hands together.

She had pretty hands, shapely. The skin looked smooth and he imagined they would feel soft. He had no doubt she worked as hard as any woman in the community, but it appeared she took care of her hands. Her nails were neatly cut and he guessed she used a lotion just like his stepmother and sisters did. And suddenly he had the strangest impulse to touch her hands, to see if they were as soft as they appeared.

"Come on," he cajoled, not quite sure what had gotten into him. He did want to talk about Jamie, but for some reason he just wanted to…to talk to her. To Abigail. This wasn't like him at all, to seek someone out. Certainly not a woman. An unmarried woman.

The evening before, Rosemary had filled him in on Abigail's husband's passing. How she had nursed him through his cancer until his death. That she had tried for years to run their farm on her own. According to his stepmother, it was only after her parents moved to Hickory Grove that she'd decided to sell her place and leave Wisconsin. And that had apparently been more about her parents than herself. Ethan had gotten the impression that June had some health issues. What they were, his stepmother hadn't said but from his couple of encounters with June, he could make a good guess. Rosemary *had*, however, expressed her opinion that Abigail had done the right thing, that her parents needed her.

"Come on, sit with me for a few minutes." Balancing his plate in one hand, Ethan waved in the direction of the yard beside the house that was planted with flowering bushes and clusters of herbs. "They've plenty of help and I've kept my eye on you. You haven't sat down since you got here at seven this morning. And we really should talk about Jamie," he added, hoping that would win her over.

She looked up at him, obviously torn.

"Ten minutes," he said. And then he walked away.

"Fine, but just five minutes," she told him. And followed.

He found a little wrought iron bench along the side

of the house, nestled between clumps of pink and white flowering azaleas. "Sit." He dropped onto the bench. "I bet you're as tired as I am."

"I'm not tired," she said.

He pushed back the brim of his straw hat and looked up at her. "You know what I mean. It will feel good to sit a minute and talk. I already have a plan worked out. Jamie's going to be reading at grade level by Christmas if he'll cooperate."

The idea of that seemed to be enough to convince her to join him because she sat down on the far end of the bench.

"What a spread," he said, looking down at the china dinner plate in his lap.

Someone had brought a church wagon from one of the larger districts. The wagons were moved from house to house where services were held. They contained tables, chairs, dishes and even silverware, enough to feed the sixty-odd people who were there, and probably then some.

He pointed at his plate. "Ham sandwich, potato salad, rice salad, macaroni and cheese, chicken salad sandwich. Which I suspect you made because it has pimentos in it." He slid a rolled napkin of silverware from his pocket. "I took too much. We can share."

She shook her head. "Thank you, but…" She smiled at him. "I can eat later with the other women."

"Forget that," he told her, surprising himself with his joviality. "If you don't help me eat this, I'll have to eat it all myself." He nodded in the direction of a silver maple whose branches were filled with leaves about to burst. "And then I'll be asleep under that tree the rest of the day."

She laughed. "Guess you shouldn't have put so much on your plate."

"Eyes bigger than my stomach, that's what my wife used to—" He halted midsentence, surprised he would mention his Mary. And to someone who was a complete stranger. Nearly.

Abigail was quiet for a moment and then said, "Phoebe told me your wife had passed. I didn't know. I'm so sorry. And I'm sorry for that comment I made to you earlier this week. I saw your beard and assumed you were married, and I was upset and—" She exhaled, looking down.

"You don't have to apologize. You already did. It's fine. Forgotten. I've seen a mother hen protect her chick in the barnyard."

"It's still not okay. For me to have said something like that when your wife was dead. I know…at least, I have some idea how that feels. What it's like. And I know it must have been hurtful. Because I know how much you must miss her," she added softly.

He stared at his plate for a moment. She did know what that was like, didn't she? Her being widowed, as well. Maybe that was why he had brought it up? Because somehow, he felt some sort of kinship to her. Sure, he had known others who had lost spouses. His own mother had died. His father had been widowed. As was Rosemary. But they were older, had thirteen children between them and somehow that seemed different. To lose a spouse when you were older. Having a wife die so young. It made you feel like you should have died with them. Sometimes wish you had.

"Look, someone put two forks in this napkin," he said trying to lighten the conversation. "I guess it was meant to be, you and I sharing this plate." He offered the fork.

She took it, which surprised him and…pleased him.

For a moment they were both quiet. Ethan cut the ham sandwich on a roll in half and then the chicken salad sandwich. He picked up half the sandwich and offered it to her. "My hands are clean. I promise. I washed up at the hand pump, soap and all."

She laughed but hesitated.

"You better take it," he warned. "Best chicken salad I've ever had. It was already almost gone when I went through the line. No way there's any left by the time the women sit down to eat." He held it out.

She accepted the sandwich and took a bite. "Do you really think you can teach Jamie to read?" she asked, and he felt himself exhaling, not realizing he'd been holding his breath, hoping she'd let him help her and her son.

Chapter Six

"I can absolutely help him. I only have a high school education, but I've done a lot of reading. A lot of studying on teaching methods and such. I think Jamie knows the sounds of most letters," Ethan explained. "And some of the digraphs."

"Digraphs?" She took a bite of the sandwich. Ethan was right. She had made the chicken salad. And brought slices of bread and soft rolls so folks could make small sandwiches and have a taste of more things. She chewed thoughtfully. She'd never heard the word *digraph*. She'd been a good student but had only completed the eighth grade. One of the things her father had taught her was to never be ashamed of admitting she didn't know something. The shame was in *not* learning, he always said. "I don't know that word. *Digraph*."

"Nobody does. It's just a fancy way of meaning the sounds certain consonants make when you put them together." He set the plate down between them on the bench. "Like *TH* in *thank*."

"*Ya*, I see. Like *ST* in *stop*." She nodded surprised to find how hungry she was. She took another bite of the sandwich and then, without being invited, dipped into the potato salad on Ethan's plate with her fork.

"Right." He took a bite of macaroni and cheese. "But Jamie doesn't understand the sounds *diphthongs* make. Those are combinations of vowels, like *EA* or *OU*. Like in *mean* or *shout*."

Abigail turned this idea over in her mind, fighting a feeling of failure. How had she not known her son was struggling? She hesitated, then glanced at him. "I feel bad. What kind of mother am I that I didn't know Jamie couldn't read?"

Ethan reached for his half of the chicken salad sandwich and took a bite. "This really is good. Want a pickle? There are pickles in there somewhere." He poked at the plate with his fork, then looked up. "You can't feel guilty about this, Abigail. Jamie's a smart boy. He had me fooled for weeks and I'm his teacher. And it's not as if you haven't had anything else to do. Your husband was sick. You were taking care of your farm." He took a napkin from the two the cutlery had been wrapped in.

She watched him, wondering how he knew so much about her. Had her mother told everyone in Hickory Grove her whole life's story? She probably should have been embarrassed about that, too. But she had to keep in mind what mattered here. And that was Jamie.

"And now you have your parents to look after," Ethan continued.

"Well, my *dat* doesn't need looking after, but my *mam*, that's another story. It's really why we came when we did. You've probably heard, she—" Abigail was quiet for a moment. "She's beginning to forget things. Sometimes words. Other times how to do things she should know how to do." She accepted the napkin he offered. "I suspect she's the one who wrapped this silverware—two napkins, two forks, one knife, one spoon. It's the sort of thing she does. My grandmother, *Mam*'s mother, got the same way. Eventually, she didn't know our names."

Abigail had no idea why she was telling Ethan all of this. She hadn't talked about her mother's memory problems with anyone but her *dat* and her next-door neighbor, Sarah, back in Wisconsin. She and Sarah had been best friends since first grade. Sarah had a husband and four children now, but no matter how busy she was, she'd always been there for Abigail: in the end with Egan when she'd been running the farm on her own, when she'd made the tough choice to move to Delaware.

"I'm sorry to hear that." Ethan wiped his mouth with his napkin. "My *grossdadi* on my mother's side got like that, too. It was hard. He used to get so upset that the sheep weren't laying eggs."

Abigail giggled, then covered her mouth with her hand. "I'm sorry. That's not funny."

"Sure it is." He grinned. "And the same grandfather used to tell me that sometimes you'd better laugh, otherwise, you'd cry."

"My mother keeps putting salt in my *dat*'s coffee every morning. And he drinks it that way because he doesn't want to upset her."

Ethan laughed as he met her gaze. "That must taste terrible."

She suppressed a giggle, having no idea what had gotten into her. She couldn't believe she was sitting here laughing with Ethan when she had been so angry with him only days before. And talking about her mother.

It was so unlike her to share with someone this way. And a man, no less. She hadn't talked to a man this way since Egan died. That thought sobered her and she took a bite of broccoli casserole from the plate. "So Jamie. You think you can help him with his…digraphs and diphthongs?" she asked.

"Positive. He just needs some one-on-one. What I was thinking, if you would be okay with it, is that Jamie could stay for a little while after school a couple of days a week. Maybe just Monday through Tuesday or Wednesday." He started on half the ham sandwich. "And only half an hour each day. I don't want to overwhelm him or make him feel like he's being punished."

"That would be fine, it would be wonderful, but—"

"But what?" He pointed at the plate between them. "Try the ham. It's good. And there are two brownies." He grimaced. "You can only have one, though. I've a bit of a sweet tooth."

"I can't eat another thing," she told him, holding her hand to her stomach. "Ethan, I appreciate your offering to help Jamie, but you have a whole schoolhouse of students five days a week. I hate to ask you to work longer days."

"You'll be doing me a favor. I feel bad that I didn't catch it the minute Jamie came to my school. And his behavior, I think a lot of it has to do with his frustration in school."

"I don't know about that. He was always a bit naughty, even as—"

"There you are!"

Phoebe approached them on the bench. "I was looking for you. Your mother, she, um…" She smiled. "She's looking for you. I think she's a little overwhelmed. So many people she doesn't know."

Abigail jumped up. "I would be so thankful if you'd help Jamie," she said to Ethan. "When do you want to start?"

"How about Monday?"

She gave a nod. "Monday." She stood there smiling at him a moment longer than seemed proper and then she hurried off after Phoebe.

Abigail walked up the schoolhouse lane to find Ethan and Jamie sitting on the steps of the cloakroom. Jamie was supposed to walk home alone after his reading lesson, but she'd decided at the last minute to meet and walk back with him. She'd been working in the garden and her father had been gone all day so she and her mother needed a break from each other. It had taken Abigail longer to hoe two rows and plant radish seeds and broccoli plants with her mother's help than without it.

Abigail had talked to her father about growing some vegetables in hills instead of rows, just to see if there was a difference in the size of the plants or the ease of keeping them watered midsummer. They had agreed. Her father had even sketched a layout of the garden with rows and hills, but June would have none of it. And no matter how many times Abigail had reminded her mother how to dig a small hole and gently place the broccoli seedlings in it, June had either buried them completely or laid them on the ground allowing the roots to dry out. By the time her father returned from his errands in Dover, Abigail had needed a few minutes to herself and walking to school seemed like the perfect opportunity to grab them.

That was what she told herself.

She'd baked cookies and wanted to give Ethan some, just as a thank-you, and if she picked up Jamie, she could give them to him. She knew she could have sent them the next day, but cookies were always so good when they were fresh. And Ethan was being so kind to be working with Jamie this way. They were on week two of his lessons and she was already seeing improvements. Ethan had sent a reader home with him and each night after supper either she or her father read with Jamie for ten minutes. At first, her son had fought her on it, but she was beginning to realize that she could be as stubborn as he could be, and she wasn't giving in on this one. If Ethan said Jamie needed ten minutes of practice five nights a week, he was going to do it.

"Excellent," Ethan said to Jamie as Abigail walked up the oyster shell driveway. He took a book from her son's lap and closed it. "You're just in time," he said, looking up at her. "All done."

"Working outside, are you?" she asked.

Ethan shrugged. "A change of scenery is good sometimes. My older girls did their social studies work sitting in the grass this afternoon." He nodded in the general direction of the back of the white clapboard schoolhouse.

Jamie popped up from the step. "Why are you here? You said I could walk home myself today." He pursed his lips. "I haven't ridden anyone's cows again."

She and Ethan both chuckled.

"Who says I came to walk you home?" Abigail approached them, carrying a little cloth shopping bag she'd made from a scrap of fabric from her mother's sewing room. It was handy for groceries or a task like this one. "I brought Ethan some cookies I made this morning." She held up the gingham bag.

"Cookies?" Jamie ran toward her. "What kind?"

"Oatmeal with chocolate chips."

"My favorite! You bring some for me?"

"*Ne.* I told you, these are for your teacher. Yours are home on the kitchen table."

"Can I run ahead?" Jamie asked excitedly.

"Please." She motioned down the driveway. "Run home. Get rid of some of that energy."

He grabbed his lunch pail from the grass and raced past her.

"I'll be right behind you," she called after him. "I have yeast rolls rising on the counter. Don't fuss with them or they'll fall. Have your cookies and milk, but then I expect you to get on your chores."

The oyster shells crunched under Jamie's feet as he ran.

"Mind the road," she hollered after him.

And then she and Ethan were alone.

She held up the bag of cookies again. "I hope you like oatmeal with chocolate chips."

"You keep bringing me cookies, and brownies and pie and I'm going to have to ask Rosemary to let out my pants." Reading primer in hand, he went up the steps. "Let me just grab my lunch pail and the keys. We'll walk home together."

Which was just what she had hoped he might say.

When Abigail took the notion to bring the cookies to Ethan herself, she realized he might have come to school that morning in his buggy, but secretly, she'd hoped he'd walked. She'd hoped they might walk together as far as her place. They'd done so twice the previous week and then again two days ago. And thinking back, she realized those had been her best days since she'd moved to Delaware.

Of course Ethan had *also* contributed to some of her worst days, but she was over that. She realized now that their bad first encounters were due to her own quick temper. Now, it seemed like she almost craved his company. Phoebe had said he was grumpier than his brothers and Abigail could see how she might get that impression. She'd seen a bit of it early on, but since Ethan had started tutoring Jamie, he'd been nothing but kind and patient. And she found that she liked talking to him. And not just about Jamie. It didn't matter the subject, whether it was his family's buggy business or farming or the school itself.

Monday on the walk home, he'd asked her opinion on the end-of-the-year school program and then he'd actually listened to her thoughts. He'd explained to her that he wanted to have a spelling bee with students being able to compete in different age groups. Of course anyone in the community would be welcome and he expected a good turnout: parents, grandparents, neighbors and family. He was also thinking about combining it with a fund-raiser, but he didn't know what kind. He said he'd thought about getting people to donate items and then auction them off on a piece of paper rather than by an auctioneer. The Englishers called it a silent auction, but he wasn't sure how the bishop would feel about that. It wasn't gambling, which was strictly forbidden, but the idea might be too newfangled. Ethan told her that Bishop Simon was pretty open to new ideas, but he also liked to caution his parishioners to take care they didn't step too far outside the boundaries their ancestors had set. He said it made it harder to find your way back if you got lost.

Abigail looked up to see Ethan coming out of the schoolhouse. He locked the door and walked down the steps toward her, putting his straw hat on his head. His face was suntanned. He must have worked outside the day before. And she noticed he'd gotten his hair cut. It looked nice, and she considered telling him so, but the idea made her feel awkward for some reason, so she didn't.

"How was your day?" she asked. The minute the words came out of her mouth, she felt her cheeks flush. She used to say the same to Egan, days when they didn't see much of each other.

Ethan didn't seem to notice her discomfort. He thought for a moment. That was something she liked about him. He was thoughtful. He chose his words carefully. She tended to respond quickly, too quickly at times, something her father, and even occasionally her husband, had criticized her for. Well, maybe not *criticized*, but gently warned of the consequences of not thinking before speaking. It was how she had gotten herself into trouble with Ethan in the first place. She looked up at him as they walked down the driveway toward the road that would lead them home. She was wearing a pale green dress and she'd put on a clean white apron before she left. The string of her white prayer *kapp*, a loop that fell to the nape of her neck, fluttered in the slight breeze.

"Mine was…good," Ethan said. "Let's see. Peter Fisher, who was never a great student, won the eighth and ninth grade spelling bee today by spelling *unforeseeable*. And…Hannah Gruber sat in her chair and did her *entire* math lesson without raising her hand a single time." He chuckled. "I love her dearly, but she constantly needs reassurance and with twenty-seven students in the class, I don't have the time. Oh—" He held up one finger. "*And* I got to eat my own lunch, for once."

"Twenty-seven students. I don't know how you do it." They started down the path, Ethan walking beside the road and she next to the drainage ditch. "And how about Jamie? How was he?"

"He was pretty good. We had an incident at lunch when the boys were supposed to be washing up and somehow they got into a water fight." He glanced at her. "One Jamie started."

She sighed. "I was hoping his behavior would be better when his reading started to improve."

"You said those cookies were for me?" Ethan pointed at the bag she was still carrying.

"*Ya.*"

"Then how about we have one." He took the bag from her, reached in and pulled out two cookies. He offered her one.

She shook her head. "*Ne.* Thank you."

"Oh, come now. Have one. Otherwise I can't. It would be rude for me to eat what looks like a delicious cookie and leave you to watch me. And they're huge." He held one up. "A meal, practically."

She laughed and accepted the cookie. She'd made them big the way her father liked them. They were the size of the palm of her hand and took more work to make than a simple drop cookie. To make one this size, she had to measure out a quarter of a cup of dough, make it into a ball, and then press it onto the cookie sheet with the bottom of a glass that had been dipped in sugar. And the cookie had to be a uniform thickness, or some would turn out overcooked, while others were undercooked.

He took a bite of his cookie. "Mmm. Excellent. I knew it would be."

She nibbled on hers, trying to suppress the pride that swelled in her chest. It was fine to do a good job at something and recognize one's accomplishments, but *hochmut* was a boastful kind of pride and one to be avoided.

"You're quite a baker, Abby." He hesitated. "Is it okay if I call you Abby? For some reason you seem more like an Abby to me than an Abigail."

She thought for a moment. The way he would. Growing up, she had always been Abigail, named after her maternal great-grandmother. And even as a child, when someone called her Abby, she politely corrected them. She had always been Abigail. But she liked the idea of him calling her Abby. There was no denying she had started to feel an attraction to Ethan, and she sensed it was mutual. She didn't want to get ahead of herself, but what if…what if they were to court? To marry even? It wouldn't happen, of course. But she liked the idea that if she remarried, and she thought she would someday, whoever she married would call her something different than Egan had. And Egan had always called her Abigail.

"No one else does," she said hesitantly. She gave a little nod. "But *ya*, you can call me Abby." She looked straight ahead, taking another bite of the cookie that truly was excellent. "I think I'd like that."

"Well, *Abby*, on the subject of your son, I do think his behavior has improved a bit." An old pickup truck approached and passed them and Ethan waited until the sound died away to continue what he was saying. "I hope you weren't expecting an overnight change. For Jamie to wake up a different boy once he could read the word *pears*."

She smiled, knowing he was teasing her a bit. But also being truthful. "*Ne*, it's only that—" She smiled and took a bite of cookie, lowering her head. "I think maybe I *was* hoping it would be an overnight cure," she said. "Because he certainly can be trouble. Saturday he decided to make mud pies and then use my clean sheets as a target. I don't know what gets into him sometimes."

"Well, I can tell you, as a teacher, there is no overnight cure for naughty boys."

She chewed her cookie, enjoying the crunchy texture of the oatmeal and the smoothness of the chocolate chunks. She never used chocolate chips for her baking. She always bought big bars of chocolate and then chopped them up. "My father says I spoil him. That that's why he misbehaves."

Ethan had finished his cookie and reached into the bag for another. "I'd have to agree with your father. That might be part of it. But I think we also have to keep in mind, as you pointed out to me that day you shouted at me—"

"I did not shout," she corrected.

"That day you *didn't* shout at me," he conceded, a teasing tone in his voice, "that Jamie's had a lot of changes in his life." He looked down at her. "He must miss his father," he said quietly.

The tenderness in Ethan's voice brought a lump up in her throat and it took a moment before she could speak again. "Did you and your wife have children?"

"We did not." Now she heard sadness in his voice. "We'd hoped God would bless us with a flock, but…" He didn't finish his sentence. He didn't need to.

She and Egan had hoped for more children, too. But it hadn't been in God's plan. That's what she always told herself when she was sad that she had only Jamie. But hearing Ethan say that he and his wife had not had children, she realized she should always be thankful for what she had and not what she didn't have. She had Jamie to remind her every day, in a good way, of the husband she had loved. Ethan had no one.

She was quiet for a moment and then said, "I don't want to pry, but… May I ask you what her name was? Your wife's?"

"Mary." He smiled as if just speaking her name brought back a good memory of her. "Mary Elizabeth. She was twenty-five. She had a seizure and died. I had just walked out of the room. One minute she was with me and the next…" He took a breath. "She was with God."

"A pretty name," Abigail mused. "I can't imagine what that was like for you, not being able to say goodbye. With Egan, once he was diagnosed with cancer of his pancreas, we knew pretty quickly that he wasn't going to survive it." She took a breath. She had no idea why she was saying these things to Ethan. She was almost in tears. But it also felt good to talk about her husband. To talk to someone who she knew understood what it was like to lose a spouse so young. "We had time to say all the things we wanted to say to each other. To say goodbye. He…he died in my arms. At home," she finished.

Both were quiet for several minutes. Just walking

side by side, lost in their own thoughts. Ethan was quiet so long that she wondered if she had overstepped some invisible boundary. Maybe he thought her sharing something so personal wasn't proper, but when he spoke, his voice was filled with a tenderness that made the backs of her eyelids sting with tears.

"Thank you for telling me about Egan." He tucked the gingham bag with three more cookies still in it into his tin lunch pail. "And thank you for listening to me tell you about Mary. I don't talk about her much."

"I don't talk about Egan. I feel like no one—" She couldn't go on.

"Understands," he finished for her. Then he looked at her. "I don't know how we got on that gloomy topic. Let's not talk about it anymore. It's too pretty a day. Did you come up with any ideas for the end-of-the-school-year program?"

"I did." A sudden excitement came over her. "I don't know how the bishop would feel about this, but back home, we used to have a pie auction. Women would bake pies and they would be auctioned off. But whoever's pie you won, you got to have dinner with the baker because she would pack a meal. You could have the children do their presentation, have the spelling bee, and then maybe there could be a time for games and visiting before the auction."

"I like that idea," Ethan said, nodding. He narrowed his gaze. "But how about a cake auction. I'm not saying I don't like pies, but I love cake."

"A cake auction would be perfect. We could put up a volleyball net. Throw horseshoes or maybe even that Englisher game with the beanbags. And then we could auction off the cakes and with them the picnic baskets.

Husbands always buy their wives' baskets of course, but it gives the singles a chance to spend some time together. A young man is sweet on a young woman—" She shrugged. "They get to spend time together."

"And—" he pointed at her "—find out what kind of cook she is."

She laughed. They were almost to her driveway already. The walk had gone by so quickly. Too quickly. "I suppose that's true." She stopped at her parents' mailbox.

He continued to walk but turned so he was walking backward. "I like the idea for the picnic supper. Let me check with the school board. I know Bishop Simon will be fine with it because we went to one over in Seven Poplars last year together. Will I see you tomorrow?"

She slid the mail out of the mailbox, looking at him questioningly. Was he asking to see her?

"If you pick up Jamie," he told her, "we can walk back together and make plans."

"Oh, I don't know if I can get away. My *dat* might need me to… I don't know," she repeated.

"Let's just plan on it and if you can't come, I'll understand."

"All right." She found herself smiling at him.

"All right. I'll see you tomorrow, Abby." Ethan turned around and walked away, whistling as he went.

Chapter Seven

Ethan was still whistling when he met up with his father in their driveway.

Benjamin waited for him, watching a stray Rhode Island Red chicken cross their path. "You certainly sound chirpy." He'd just left the harness shop where there were two buggies, a horse and wagon, and two pickup trucks parked in the gravel parking lot. He was walking up the lane toward the house, limping slightly.

Ethan shrugged, switching his lunch pail from one hand to the other, seriously considering having another cookie. It would be hours before suppertime, and they had been so delicious. "I had a good day. One of my students' mothers brought me cookies." He slowed his pace so he could walk beside his father. "To thank me for spending some extra time after school with her son. He's struggling with reading."

Ethan felt no need to go into any more detail. It wasn't necessary that others know Jamie couldn't read. It would be righted soon enough. He didn't want to cause embarrassment to his student or Abby.

"She brought you cookies?" His father stopped and

looked up at Ethan, who was several inches taller than he was. "Who?"

"Abigail Stolz. Daniel King's daughter."

"The one you had trouble with?"

Ethan nodded.

A smile tugged at the corners of his father's mouth. "Nice girl. Pretty. Good cook, Rosemary says. Abigail gave her a recipe for brown sugar tarts. Of course I know you've had trouble with her boy." He narrowed his gaze and he waggled his finger. "Karl Lapp had a tale to tell about that one. You marry a woman with a child, you become that child's father. His behavior problems become yours."

"Who said anything about marrying anyone?" Ethan opened his arms wide, his lunch pail swinging in his hand. "She brought me cookies."

"A way to a man's heart…" Benjamin patted his round belly. "I took one bite of your mother's *rosina boi* at a harvest dinner and decided there and then she was the woman for me. Walked right up to her and asked her to walk out with me. We married six months later."

"You did *not* marry my mother merely on the basis of how good a raisin pie she could bake," Ethan argued. "And Jamie is just a little boy." He shrugged. "Little boys are mischief-makers. I know I was when I was his age. Remember that time I took those watercolor paints *Grossmami* gave me and painted *Mam*'s white goat. Gave her spots?"

His father chuckled at the memory, then cocked his head as he resumed walking. His tone became serious. "Abigail you say… Lost her husband a couple of years ago, didn't she?"

Ethan nodded. "She did. It was cancer. They lived

in Wisconsin. After he passed, she ran the farm for a while before it got to be too much. It wasn't until June and Daniel moved here to be closer to his brother that she decided it was time to sell her farm."

His father started toward the house again, his forehead crinkling. "Who's Daniel's brother again?"

Ethan had to think for a minute. "A King over in Seven Poplars. His boy married Hannah Hartman's daughter Susanna. She and her husband live with Hannah and Albert and both have Down's."

His father snapped his fingers. "Right, right. Ebben King. His son David King rides along with Albert sometimes when he makes veterinary calls." He touched the brim of his straw hat. "Wears a paper crown from that burger place all the time. They were out here last fall to have a look at Toby when he got wrapped up in that bit of wire and cut his hock."

"*Ya*, that's him," Ethan agreed, ambling so his father could keep up with him. In the distance, he could hear the sounds of lambs bleating and a guinea hen that must have had her feathers in a ruffle. "I think Ebben is a younger brother to Daniel. I heard that Ebben convinced his brother to move to Delaware for the better climate. Not as much snow to shovel here in the winter as Wisconsin."

"Or upstate New York." His father shook his head. "We sure did shovel our share of snow when we lived there. And then some."

"We sure did," Ethan agreed.

They walked a piece, just enjoying the peacefulness of the afternoon, and then his father spoke again. "You want to ask her to join us Sunday?"

"Ask who?" Ethan drew his head back, wondering what he'd missed.

"The King girl. Stolz. Abigail." His father stroked his graying beard. "It's a visiting day. No church. Weather is supposed to be good. Rosemary thought she'd make a barrel of iced tea, maybe some lemonade, and we'd sit outside. This morning she had Jacob bring the outdoor chairs from the barn and hose them down."

It was on the tip of Ethan's tongue to say of course he wasn't going to invite Abby to visit on Sunday. He didn't invite women anywhere for visiting Sundays or for anything else. But then he realized that he might actually like that. To see Abby this Sunday. It would give them more time to talk about the end-of-the-school-year program. The walk home from the school to her place was too short. An hour together and they could work out all of the details.

But if he was truthful with himself, the fact was that even if they didn't have the school event to plan, he'd enjoy having a glass of tea with her on Sunday afternoon. He might even take her to see the new buggy he and his father were working on. If she'd be interested.

"You should invite the whole family," Ethan's father continued. "I like Daniel from what I can tell. Them still being new to Hickory Grove, it would be the neighborly thing to do." He halted for a moment, breathing heavily.

"You okay, *Dat*?"

Ethan's father rubbed his right hip. "My arthritis is giving me a fit this week. Rosemary wanted me to stay around the house today. Or at least take a cane."

"But you were stubborn," Ethan said.

Benjamin gave a huff and limped forward. "Too much work to be done to be sitting around the house. I should have been at the plow in the garden hours ago. Headed that way now. To hitch up Blue and Carter."

"You already plowed the garden weeks ago."

"Rosemary wants a couple more rows. Wants to plant some fancy kind of sweet corn Edna Fisher was telling her about." He muttered something under his breath that Ethan didn't catch. "I don't know why I bought a place this big. Rosemary told me we didn't need all this land, but I said I wanted it for our sons. Our daughters, too, if any of our girls wanted to raise their families here." He chuckled. "She teased me about being an old woman, wanting all my chicks under one roof."

"I don't know that that will happen. Rosemary's Lovey and her family are settled at his place down the road. And Mary's in New York. I don't see her and Amos and their brood moving south anytime soon."

His father shrugged. "Never know. Your sister and her husband might get to an age when they are tired of shoveling snow, too. Mary said in a letter last week that she was never so glad to see the first spring thaw. Said they had a hundred and seventy inches of snowfall this year. Glad we left that all behind, but Rosemary was right. I tried to tackle too much here. All this land, the upkeep of a big house, the outbuildings." He threw up his hand. "Then I got it in my head to open a harness shop again. Rosemary asked me why. I told her for the same reason we needed all this acreage. For our children. To give them opportunities for an honest day's work." He looked up at Ethan. "It's a good thing I have you here, son. I don't know what I'd do without you."

"What are you talking about? Doing without me," Ethan grumbled. "I'm right here, *Dat*."

"Right here with no wife. No grandchildren to see me through my old age."

Ethan started to say he wasn't going around that hoop again, but he held his tongue. Instead, he glanced up at the sun, still bright in the sky. "Why don't I get those rows plowed for you and keep you out of hot water with Rosemary. Maybe you could have a look at that seat upholstery I was working on." He pulled the brim of his straw hat down a bit to block the glare of the sun, now lower on the horizon.

His father stopped again, seeming thankful for the break. "What's wrong with it?"

"I don't know. Folds aren't right. Might be the leather, but I'm afraid it's the padding beneath." Ethan gestured impatiently. "Which means I have to pull out all the tacks, lift the leather without tearing it and fix the padding."

His father rubbed his hip, glancing in the direction of the garden beside the house. Part of it was fenced in, but now they were planting outside that area. He and Rosemary were trying to decide whether or not to extend the perimeter of the fence or just plant some crops beyond it this year and take their chances with the critters. "You wouldn't mind plowing? Four rows are all she needs."

"Don't mind at all," Ethan said. "If you don't mind having a look at that buggy seat."

"All right, then." As his father turned to go, he patted him on the shoulder. "Like I said. Don't know what I'd do without you."

Abigail walked beside Ethan up the lane of his family's farm. It was late afternoon and sun had begun to shift in the sky, but it was still warm on her face and she could smell the freshness in the air that spring brought with it. Ethan was walking beside her, explaining the difference between metal-rimmed and rubber-rimmed buggy wheels. She was only half listening, though she'd asked him the question. Instead, her mind kept wandering as she enjoyed the pleasant cadence of his voice.

Ethan had invited her family over for the afternoon. It was a visiting Sunday for their church district. That meant that instead of spending a full day in one of their homes listening to a preacher's sermon, praying and singing hymns, they used the hours for outings to see friends, neighbors or family members. Or hosted. Because Abigail and her family were new to the community and because of her mother's situation, they hadn't even had anyone over. They'd either stayed home or gone visiting since her and Jamie's arrival. Though on the wagon ride over to the Millers, her father had said he would like to have his brother's family over, and maybe a few of their neighbors. He'd asked Abigail if she'd be up to it and she'd agreed. It was only a matter of deciding when.

As Ethan went on explaining the advantages of rubber-rimmed wheels, a smoother, quieter ride being one of them, she dared a glance up at him. He was wearing his Sunday clothes: dark pants and vest with a white shirt with the long sleeves rolled casually to his elbows. Instead of the usual wide-brimmed black felt hat worn to church, he sported his everyday straw hat. His hair was neat, his beard cut shorter than it had been earlier in the week and his hands were clean, his nails neatly trimmed.

Sometimes on visiting Sunday, folks just wore everyday clothes. Abigail was glad that she'd chosen her more formal black dress with a white apron and white cape that went over her shoulders and pinned into her apron. Because of the warmth of the day and casualness of the gathering, she'd just worn a white prayer *kapp* and forgone the black bonnet. But she'd chosen her church *kapp* with the strings hanging in the front, rather than the more modern single loop in the back.

Ethan had sought her out the moment her family arrived. The two of them had been talking all afternoon. She was the one who, a few minutes ago, had suggested they should join the others in the backyard. They had been gone at least an hour. First, he'd taken her to see the harness shop, which she'd never visited, then to the back of the building to where he and his father were building buggies. It wasn't that she wanted to return to the group of women under the trees talking recipes and babies. She was enjoying her time with Ethan.

They'd talked about the end-of-the-school-year fundraiser and agreed to have the cake and picnic basket auction. He'd already gotten the okay from the bishop. They'd talked about Jamie's progress as well and discussed the possibility of continuing tutoring over the summer in the hopes he would be caught up with the other students his age by the time school began in the fall.

But Abigail was beginning to feel guilty about abandoning her responsibilities and felt the need to return to her family. Ethan had assured her that Jamie couldn't get into too much trouble with Jesse by his side. But she was also concerned about her mother. Her mother wasn't as comfortable being with strangers anymore. She'd refused invitations to go visiting and to join a quilting circle. Her mother's excuse had been that there was too much work to be done in the house and garden,

but Abigail had a suspicion her mother was turning into
a homebody because that was where she was the most
comfortable. When she got outside her own surround-
ings, she began to forget people's names, words for
common objects, simple tasks. She stressed over her forgetfulness and that seemed to make her more forgetful.

Then, there was the issue of decorum. Single men
and single women weren't supposed to spend hours
alone talking. Even at their age, and even though they
were both widowed, the tradition was to have a chap-
erone. It could be anyone, an elderly aunt, another couple, even a child. It was Abby's opinion that such rules
were a bit silly. After all, she and Ethan weren't teenagers. And they both had been baptized long ago. Neither
would ever say or do something inappropriate. Still, she
was new to the community and she didn't want her behavior to reflect poorly on her parents.

She stole another glance at Ethan. He was a handsome man: larger than his brothers and father, taller.
Not stout like Benjamin, but muscular. More muscular
than Egan had been. Her thoughts drifted back to her
husband, but the stab of pain she had felt for so long
wasn't there today. She'd been feeling it ease for the
last six months or so. It wasn't that she didn't still love
Egan, but she'd noticed a subtle difference. Life without him was getting, if not easier, more comfortable.

"Do you still miss her?" Abigail asked suddenly.

Ethan halted and looked down at her. For a long moment he didn't reply. Maybe he didn't know who she
was referring to, but then he answered.

"My wife? *Ya.* Every day."

She nodded thoughtfully. "Me, too. I knew Egan
from my school days. His family was in our church dis-

trict. We saw each other growing up, through our teens. He was always there." She lifted her gaze. "Where did you meet Mary?"

He stroked his beard, seeming to consider whether or not to tell her. "She was visiting a neighbor of ours. We met at singing the first week she arrived. I was there chaperoning more than attending the singing. I was getting a little old for that sort of thing."

A pure white cat with red eyes walked lazily down the lane toward them and they both watched it for a moment.

"Mary was only supposed to stay with her cousins for two weeks, but she stayed four. Which turned to six." Ethan was still watching the cat. "We'd known each other two months and three days when I asked her to marry me."

The cat walked up to Ethan and rubbed against his pant leg. Abigail could hear it purring loudly. "So you didn't court for long?"

He shook his head. "That was spring. We married in November. Most weddings in our community up in New York were in November." He surprised her by squatting down to pet the cat. "Snowball," he said.

"What's that?"

"The cat. Her name is Snowball." He stroked the cat's fluffy white coat. "One of my students brought her to me this winter. She's an albino. His parents were going to drown her, so he smuggled her out of his barn and brought her to school. He couldn't bear the thought. He begged me to take her, so I did."

Abigail smiled faintly, touched by his tenderness. "Egan and I courted for some time. He wasn't ready to marry. Still sowing his oats. We saw each other all the time, but we'd agreed that if we ever met someone else we were interested in, we were free to get to know him or her."

"That ever happen?" He scratched the cat behind her ears.

"*Ne.* One day Egan just came to me and said it was time. He said he loved me. That he'd always loved me, and that God was leading him to become a husband, a father and he wanted to marry me." The cat moved on to her, purring and rubbing against her ankle. She crouched down to pet it. "We took our time marrying because we thought we'd have a lifetime together," she said softly. When she looked up, he was studying her intently.

"I know what you mean about thinking we had a whole life ahead of us," he said. "We thought the same thing. We had so many plans."

Abigail felt a scratchiness behind her eyelids. She stroked the cat. She had no idea why she had brought up the subject of their spouses. Had God led her here? She'd been praying so hard these last few months for Him to show her the way out of this loneliness. Was He leading now? Was that how she had ended spending the afternoon with her son's schoolmaster? The idea seemed outlandish, yet maybe not. "I was so lost after Egan died."

"Me, too. After I lost Mary."

"And I felt so alone, even though I had my *mam* and *dat* and Jamie."

He gestured in the direction of the house. "We've got two kitchen tables to seat us all at suppertime. And I still feel lonely."

"For Mary?" she asked.

He nodded. "For Mary but also for—" He sighed. "For a life of my own. Children," he finished, emotion in his voice.

She met his solemn gaze and smiled. "I understand."

"Most don't. But I think you do," he said. Slowly he came to his feet and she did the same. And for what seemed like a long time, he just stood, looking into her eyes.

Abigail felt like she should say something, but she didn't know what.

"Ethan!" a voice rang out.

Abigail and Ethan both looked up the driveway in the direction of the voice. It was Jesse and he was coming at them at a dead run. "Ethan! Abigail! Come quick!"

Abigail's first thought was that Jamie had been hurt. Or done something bad again. She hurried toward Jesse.

The boy cupped his hands around his mouth. "Benjamin sent me to fetch you both!"

"What is it?" Ethan called, taking long strides, passing her. "What's wrong?"

"Is it Jamie?" Abigail walked fast, nearly breaking into a run. Last she'd seen her son, he was headed toward the pond with Jesse and some other boys from down the road. Her son knew how to swim, and he'd begged to be allowed to go with the older boys. Her father had said he would be fine. Ethan, too, but what if—

"Jesse!" Ethan said sharply. "Did something happen to Jamie?"

"Ne." Jesse panted, almost to them now. "It's June."

Abigail clutched her chest with one hand. "My mother?" She couldn't imagine what could be wrong with her mother. She was healthy as a horse. It was her father who'd had to see a cardiologist once. "Is she sick?"

"Ne. Not sick." Jesse came to a halt and leaned over to rest his hands on his knees, panting hard. "She's missing," he finally managed as he gulped for air. "We can't find her anywhere on the farm."

Chapter Eight

Abigail found her father in front of the Millers' barn, buckling their horse's harness. "You lost *Mam*?" she questioned sharply.

Her father glanced at her, then at Jamie who was standing on the other side of their bay. Thankfully, at least she didn't have to worry about her son at the moment.

"Check that side," her father told Jamie. He looked back at her. "I didn't *lose* your mother." He threw up one hand, clearly upset. "She was sitting under the trees with the women. She was fine. Having a good time, I think. I just walked down to the horse pasture with Benjamin to check on his mare that's about to foal. She was right there." He pointed in the direction of the picnic tables and chairs under the shade of a big silver poplar tree.

When Abigail had walked down to the harness shop with Ethan, there had been half a dozen women sitting there, surrounded by small children, talking about the best stitches to use on particular quilt patterns. Her mother *had* seemed fine. She had actually been excited to go to the Millers' and had seemed relatively at ease when Abigail had left her seated beside Edna Fisher.

Now the women who had been sitting in the chairs drinking lemonade and iced tea were bustling around the yard, children trailing behind them, calling, "June? June!"

"Check the garden again," one of Ethan's stepsisters, Abigail didn't know which, called to another. "And around the pond."

Abigail returned her attention to her father. She felt terrible. She shouldn't have been gone so long with Ethan. She should have stayed at her mother's side. It was her duty. "Are you sure she's not in the house?" she asked, pressing her hand to her forehead.

"She's not in the house," her father replied, running his hand over the bay's bridle.

"In the bathroom?" Abigail asked, feeling more anxious by the second.

"Not in the bathroom." Her father was growing terser with her by the moment. "And nowhere that we can find her on the property. We've already looked. Everyone has looked. And called her and looked again."

"How long has she been missing?" Abigail exclaimed.

"I don't know. Half an hour, maybe." Her father looked to Jamie. "Good on that side?"

"Ya, Grossdadi."

"Goot. Hop up." He gestured to the wagon.

"Dat!" Abigail exclaimed. "Where are you going?"

"Abigail," Ethan said, startling her.

She hadn't even heard him approach.

"No need to panic," Ethan said calmly.

"No need to *panic*?" She swung around to face him, her tone growing shrill. "You don't understand. My *mam,* she doesn't—" She lowered her voice. "She gets confused. I told you that."

"I understand, but it's going to be all right." He brushed his hand across her shoulder blade. "She couldn't have gotten far."

It was only the briefest touch, but Abigail felt the flutter of anxiety in her chest ease. There was something about the gentle tone of his voice that calmed her. She took a deep breath. "You're right. She can't be far. She hasn't been gone long and she's not much of a walker anymore," she said, trying to gain her composure.

Ethan turned to her father. "Jesse just told me that one of the Fisher boys saw June walking across the field, headed for the road. They didn't think anything of it."

Abigail looked at her father. "She must have just gone home."

"That's what I'm thinking," Ethan agreed.

Abigail spotted Jesse leading Ethan's horse and wagon into the barnyard as chickens scattered to get out of their way.

"Here you go, all hitched and ready to go," Jesse called to his big brother.

Ethan grabbed the reins. "You should stay here, in case she comes back here," he told Abigail.

"I'm not staying here! She could be walking along the road. You know how fast those cars go!" She hurried toward her father's wagon.

"Jamie, you stay here. Keep a look out for your *grossmami,*" Ethan ordered. "Your *grossdadi* and *mam* will head for home."

"Where are you going?" Abigail asked as Jamie jumped down and she clambered up into her father's wagon. The moment her black Sunday shoes touched the floorboards, her father tightened the reins and eased their bay backward.

"I'm going to follow you." Ethan leaped up into his wagon and remained standing as he took a rein in each hand.

"Why are you following us?" Abigail called over her shoulder as her father pulled around.

"In case she's not there," Ethan called back.

Abigail sat down hard on the seat as the wagon lurched forward, understanding Ethan's meaning. He was taking his wagon in case her mother hadn't gone home. In case she really was lost.

When Ethan saw Abby come running from her house, he knew June wasn't there. And she hadn't been on the road between his place and the Kings', else they would have seen her. If she'd cut across the field as the Fisher boy said, if she was headed home, they should have seen her on the road.

"She isn't here!" Abby called as she ran toward his wagon.

Despite the seriousness of the situation, he smiled inwardly. There weren't many Amish women her age who would run, no matter what the situation. Certainly not on a Sabbath day. He knew his Mary wouldn't have. But there was something about the strength of Abby's love for her mother, for her family that touched him. She would run to look for her mother. She'd go head-to-head with a schoolmaster over her son. The fact that she had been wrong about the situation with Jamie didn't matter. What impressed him was the fierceness of her love for her child, for her whole family.

"*Dat*'s going to look around, but she's not here. If she were, Boots wouldn't have been on her chair on the porch." Reaching his wagon, she hitched up her skirt.

Ethan threw out his hand and she accepted it, leaping up into his wagon. "Who's Boots?" he asked.

"*Dat*'s dog." She pointed at their border collie. "She's not allowed on the chairs. *Mam* won't have it. Boots only does it when *Mam* isn't home."

The black-and-white dog was now on the porch steps barking at him, but with no great menace.

"Drive," she ordered, releasing Ethan's hand.

It was odd, but he almost felt a sense of loss when she let go. All these years since Mary's death, Ethan hadn't been able to bring himself to even think about another woman and suddenly, there was Abby. Abby whom he wanted to talk to. Wanted to be with.

"Drive," she repeated, dropping onto the wooden bench seat as she gestured forward.

"Where we going?" he asked, loosening the reins, but still on his feet. Butterscotch was a mare who had always taken a light hand. At the slightest urging, she broke into a trot, seeming to sense the importance of the situation.

"I don't know." Abby shook her head, her *kapp* strings swinging. "Back to the road. Maybe she was trying to go home and missed our driveway."

He'd noticed Abby had worn her church prayer *kapp* today, not an everyday *kapp* like some of the women, like his stepsisters. The movement of the starched linen strings seemed almost like tendrils of Abby's blond hair and he felt a heaviness in his chest, an urge to protect her, to protect her family. To make everything all right, just as he had promised it would be.

He eased onto the bench seat beside her.

"Let's keep going up Cherry Road, in the direction of the main road." She pressed her hands to the seat to steady herself. "Maybe she—I don't know—I don't know—"

She sounded as if she was close to tears and without thinking, Ethan reached down and covered her hand with his. "I'll find her," he promised.

Abby looked up at him. She wasn't crying, but her eyes were moist. Blue eyes, big blue eyes. He swallowed hard. Then took the reins firmly in both hands and urged Butterscotch to go faster.

And find her he did. They were riding down the road at a trot, him scanning one side of the road and the fields, Abby the other. They'd passed neighbors from another church district, the Yoders from over near Rose Valley, and called to them as they passed, asking if they might have seen June. George and Eda Yoder and their passel of little ones had promised to keep their eyes out for her.

Ethan spotted June as they were passing the school. He almost missed her, but out of the corner of his eye, he saw movement behind the schoolhouse. He made a U-turn right in the middle of the two-lane road.

"What is it?" Abby grabbed the side of the wagon as Ethan whipped it around and it rocked precariously. "Is it *Mam*? Did you see her?"

He came to his feet, slowing Butterscotch down so as not to startle June. If it *was* June, which he was pretty certain it was. What other seventy-year-old woman dressed in Sunday church black, a white apron and white cape would be swinging on a child's swing?

"I think so. Maybe," Ethan said under his breath as he turned into the school's driveway.

Butterscotch stepped high, the oyster shells familiar under her feet. As they came around the corner of the schoolhouse, Abby saw her mother at the same moment that Ethan did.

"Mam!" Abby cried out. She barely waited until the wagon had rolled to a stop to leap down and rush across the grass.

Sighing with relief, Ethan took his time tying down the reins and climbing down from the wagon. He didn't bother to tie Butterscotch up. He knew she wouldn't go anywhere.

"Mam, we've been looking for you." Abby wasn't running now, but she was walking fast, her *kapp* strings fluttering behind her again. "What are you doing here?"

June King was a sight to behold: a tiny, frail bird of a woman dressed all in black and white. Except for her shoes. She'd shed those, and petite bare feet poked out from beneath her dress as she swung forward on the swing. It was a child's swing, chains and a canvas seat, set at a height for Ethan's younger students, but the right height for June who couldn't have been five feet tall.

June gazed at the both of them, a slight smile of something that couldn't be described any other way but satisfaction on her face. And swung higher.

"Mam," Abby said, the relief in her voice turning to frustration. "What are you doing here?" she repeated.

June pumped her legs and flew backward. "Swinging."

Ethan couldn't resist a smile, but he dropped it as Abby looked back at him.

Abby walked closer. "We looked everywhere for you, *Mam.* I thought you were lost or hurt or—"

"Not lost or hurt, as you can see," June responded.

"What are you doing here? Why are you swinging?"

"Haven't been on a swing in years. Not since my

school days. The ladies and I were talking about our school days. About the desks all lined up. Learning our numbers. Swinging on a swing at recess. At my school, we didn't have a fancy swing like this." She pointed at the rusty metal swing set a member of the school board had procured from one of the public schools in Dover when they remodeled their playgrounds some years ago. "Ours hung from a tree. Pin oak, I think it was," June mused. "I wanted to swing again."

"*Mam*, you have to get off the swing," Abby said, pointing at the grass.

"Why?" June asked. "I like it. It's fun. You should try it."

Ethan had to look away not to smile this time. He knew it wasn't funny. He understood why Abby and Daniel and everyone else had been so concerned when June had gone missing. He had already gathered from things Abby had said, and from June's behavior the couple times he'd seen her, that she was suffering from some form of dementia. It was evident not so much in her forgetfulness but in her lack of the normal inhibitions most adults had. But…the joy in June's voice just made him want to smile. The fact that she could find such pure pleasure in something so simple as a child's swing lightened his heart.

"*Mam*, get down now." Abby pointed at the ground. "We have to go. *Dat*'s waiting for you." She stepped even closer, close enough for June to almost touch her with her little bare feet when she swung forward. "He was worried. We didn't know where you were."

When June continued to swing, Abigail said tersely, "*Mam*, it's *Sunday*."

With a huff, June leaned backward, allowing the swing to slow.

Abby picked up her mother's black leather shoes and black stockings that were lying in the grass. As she gathered them, Ethan watched her with admiration. She was a good daughter. Certainly, a good mother. He'd enjoyed the afternoon with her. Enjoyed it far more than he had anticipated.

"Let's go home," Abby told her mother and the two women walked toward the wagon.

Ethan helped June onto the back bench seat and waited, his eyes averted as Abby put her mother's stockings on for her and then her shoes and tied them.

"Straighten your *kapp, Mam*," Abby said when she was done with the business of the shoes. Then she turned to Ethan and looked up at him. "I don't know how to thank you."

"No need to thank me. I'm just glad she's okay," he said softly.

"Cookies or brownies?" There was a playfulness in her voice. "Or maybe a batch of my blondies. You'd like them. I make them with macadamia nuts and white chocolate chunks."

"She makes a decent blondie," June piped up from the back of the wagon. "But I like her *mandelplaettchen* better. No one makes better almond wafers in all of Wisconsin. That's what all the ladies say."

Neither Ethan nor Abby looked back at June.

"I'll take the blondies," he said.

Abigail gave a nod, smiling back at him. "Blondies it is."

The sound of a buggy approaching caught her attention and she glanced up. It was the Fishers: Edna, John and more children in their wagon than seemed possible to fit in the rear. They slowed, then seeing June, waved as they passed.

"Good to see all's well, ends well," Edna called.

Abby waved back, thankful the Fishers didn't stop to ask where they had found her mother. She didn't know if her mother would be embarrassed by the truth, but even if her mother wouldn't be, Abigail wasn't ready for questions. She wasn't ready to discuss her mother's situation with people she barely knew.

They drove the last half mile in comfortable silence. Then, just as Ethan went to make the turn into their driveway, her mother said from the back seat, "Supper."

"We already planned our supper, *Mam*. We're having the rest of that roaster we made yesterday," Abby said over her shoulder. "And creamed cabbage and greens with mustard sauce. We picked those nice greens yesterday, you and I."

"I'm not asking what we're having for supper tonight," her mother declared indignantly. She leaned forward, thrusting herself between Ethan and her daughter. She looked at Ethan. "Come to supper. Not tomorrow night. Not the next night. The next one." She touched her hand to her forehead. "I don't know what day that is, offhand, but that day. You know which one I mean."

"Wednesday," Abby supplied, not sure if she liked the idea or not of having Ethan to supper. It certainly seemed like the right thing to do. Without Ethan's help, she didn't know how long it would have taken to find her mother.

Nonetheless, once she issued the invitation to supper, she fretted. There was no telling what her mother might say or do. Her mother might be perfectly fine. But she might also come to the supper table wearing her winter wool cloak, or worse, an undergarment over the top of her clothes. Or she might tell a tale of when she grew up living in a cookie house. It had happened before. It was a realistic concern.

"Wednesday," her mother repeated, still addressing Ethan. "Come Wednesday. Have supper, then you and my daughter can take a walk down to the pond." She poked him with one of her tiny, bony fingers. "It's a nice place for walking, our pond."

Abby was sure her face turned bright red. She couldn't look at Ethan. *"Mam,"* she chastised. "Ethan doesn't want to walk to the pond. You invited him for supper."

They turned into the driveway and suddenly Abigail remembered her son. "Jamie," she said. She'd been so caught up in the drama of her missing mother, and then the whole thing with Ethan that she had forgotten about her son. She brought her hands to her cheeks. "He's still at your place," she told Ethan.

"I'll go back, fetch him and bring him home." He glanced at her as they rode up the driveway. "Unless you want to ride back to my place with me. I can bring you both back."

Abigail was tempted. She'd had such a nice day with him that she hated to see it end. But then she thought better of it. She needed to get her mother safely home and rested. At her age, her mother had to be exhausted to have walked so far. And then all that swinging. And Abigail needed to get supper on the table. The whole family had to be famished. "I'd best stay here and get her settled." She tilted her head in her mother's direction. "Would you mind fetching Jamie? I know he could probably walk but I don't think my heart could take it tonight. I've already had enough excitement for one Sabbath."

His mouth turned up in a half smile. "*Ne*, I don't mind a bit."

As they came up the drive, Abigail's father hurried down the porch steps, relief on his face. Boots barked and raced for the wagon wheels.

"Found her. She's fine," Ethan called as he pulled up at the porch.

"June," Abigail's father said, his eyes red. "Where have you been?" He reached up and lifted her down from the wagon.

"The schoolmaster is coming for supper," Abigail's mother announced as her husband ushered her toward the house.

Abigail remained in the wagon, watching her parents go into the house and then she turned to Ethan. "I can't thank you enough for helping us." She shook her head. "She's never wandered off before but something terrible could have—" She exhaled, considering how much more to say, but then blurted, "*Dat*... I think he has his head buried in the sand. He says she's fine but makes excuses for her all the time. Blames himself or us for her mistakes. I keep telling him there's something wrong, but he gets upset when I even try to talk about it. He says I don't know what I'm talking about. That she's just forgetful."

Ethan rubbed his thumbs along the smooth leather of the reins. "Has she been to a doctor about this?"

She exhaled. "*Ne*. Like I said, *Dat* doesn't think there's anything wrong with her."

"Can I make a suggestion?"

She looked up at him. She found it so interesting that he didn't seem much like the man she had argued with at the end of her driveway a month ago. This side of him she had seen today had been so kind, so patient.

"What should I do?" she asked.

"Make an appointment for your *mam* with a neurologist. That's a doctor that knows about the brain. She can be tested."

She considered the idea. While her parents weren't beyond seeing a doctor, they had no health insurance. The Amish didn't believe in health insurance. A person paid their own doctor's bills, or if there was an accident or a severe illness like her Egan's cancer, the entire community pitched in. "That could be expensive. This friend of *Mam*'s back in Wisconsin, she had, you, know—" she waved her hand "—some kind of scans. It was costly."

"I can get the name of a good neurologist Rosemary knows about. A friend of hers over in Rose Valley used her."

"A woman neurologist?" Abigail asked in surprise.

He shrugged. "I guess so. Rosemary's friend talked to the doctor about the costs and the doctor did some tests, but not others. I think a neurologist can talk to someone, ask questions and make a good guess if the problem is just forgetfulness or something else. Like Alzheimer's, that's what my *grossdadi* had. You've heard of that, right?"

She nodded.

"Then there might be some kind of medicine your *mam* could take. I don't think there's a cure, but it might help her."

Abigail exhaled. The idea of convincing her father her mother needed to see a doctor, then tracking down the name and phone number of a neurologist, making an appointment, and getting there seemed overwhelming. But she didn't want to tell Ethan that. She didn't want him to think she was helpless.

Seeming to sense her hesitation, he said, "I could find out the doctor's name. And we've got a phone at the harness shop. You could walk over and make the call."

"I could do that," she agreed slowly.

"And I can give you the names of some drivers we use. Or even…" He hesitated. "I'd go with you if you wanted. If…your *dat* didn't want to. School will be out soon and then I'll just be working on the farm." He opened his arms. "It wouldn't be a problem."

"Thank you." She offered a quick smile. "I'll talk to *Dat*. And to *Mam*," she added. "She knows something's wrong. She gets frustrated sometimes when she can't remember things. She might want to go see a doctor." She clasped her hands looking down at them. "Thank you," she said again softly. "For everything." She stood to get out of the wagon. "So I guess we'll see you for supper." She stepped to the ground and looked up at him. "Wednesday."

"Wednesday supper it is," he agreed. "But I hope I'll see you before that," he called as he pulled away.

Abigail's father was waiting for her on the porch steps, his hands in his pockets, watching Ethan pull away. "You walking out with him?" he asked.

Abigail looked up, her skirt bunched in her hands. "What? *Ne*." She shook her head. "What would give you that idea?"

Her father continued to watch Ethan go down the

driveway. "You've been seeing a lot of him. Walking home together from school most days. And you were gone more than an hour today with him over at his place."

Abigail stopped in front of her father. "He was showing me the harness shop. And…and where he and his *dat* are making buggies," she said suddenly flustered. "We talked about Jamie's progress."

"Showing you the buggy he's making," her father repeated, seeming amused.

"*Ya, Dat.* I wanted to see it." She brushed past him, annoyed he would even think such a thing. What had given him the idea Ethan would be interested in courting her?

He turned to watch her go. "Well, if he didn't ask you to court him, only be a matter of time."

Abigail looked up to see her *mam* in the doorway clap her hands together and squeal with delight. "Abigail's courting the schoolmaster!" she exclaimed, bouncing on the balls of her feet the way Jamie did sometimes. "We're going to have a wedding!"

"*Mam!*" Abigail opened the screen door. "No one's courting anyone. No one said anything about a wedding. *Dat?*" She turned to him, her expression pleading.

But he just laughed and shrugged as he followed them into the kitchen. "You know your *mam*. I can't do a thing with her."

Chapter Nine

"I don't understand," Jamie whined to his mother from down the hall. "Why is *Tietscher* coming for supper?"

Abigail had sent him to wash his face and hands before supper. Ethan would be there any moment and for some reason she was all a jitter. She had nothing to be nervous about. Her mother had invited a neighbor to supper, that was all this was. And she knew how to make supper for a neighbor; she'd done it a hundred times. The table was set, she'd just pulled the *schnitz un kneff* out of the oven and the whole kitchen smelled like the smoked pork and dried apple dish. She had hot potato salad resting on the back of the stove, along with a saucepan of lima beans with bacon to be reheated. The freshly baked buttermilk biscuits were already on the table. She just had to grab the apple butter and the blackberry jam she'd brought from Wisconsin out of the icebox. It was a good weeknight supper. Actually, more suitable for a dinner. But on weekdays, during the school year, her family tended to eat like Englishers and have their heavier meal at the end of the day rather than midday, so Jamie could be included.

Abigail fussed with her apron, worried now that it was too much, such a big meal. That it would seem as if she was trying to show off her cooking skills. Would he think her too prideful? She'd even made two desserts not knowing which he would prefer: a fruit pudding and a German nut cake. She knew he had a sweet tooth, but one dessert probably would have been enough.

"*Mam*, why is *Tietscher* coming to supper?" Jamie repeated, walking into the kitchen. His hands were still wet, and he had missed a smudge of dirt on his face, but he smelled as if he had at least used soap.

Abigail handed her son a dish towel. "Dry your hands." She went to the stove to turn the lima beans back on. Like many Amish homes, they had both a woodstove and a gas stove for cooking, but she preferred the gas stove. The temperatures on the stove top and the oven were more predictable. Her mother, however, preferred the woodstove and had used it to bake corn bread muffins which Abigail was afraid weren't going to be edible. Her mother had added too much salt to the batter and then burned the bottoms. Abigail had considered throwing the muffins to the chickens and just serving the biscuits, but her mother was so pleased with having made them that she couldn't bring herself to do it.

Maybe, Abigail thought to herself, she could move the basket to the far end of the table and hope, with all of the other food on the table, Ethan wouldn't take one.

"*Mam*." Jamie drew out the word.

Abigail looked down at her son in exasperation. "Your grandmother invited him. As a...thank-you." Originally, Ethan had been invited for supper Wednesday, but he'd ended up postponing until Friday because he'd gone with his father to a doctor's appointment Wednesday and had had another commitment Thursday night.

"What's she thanking him for?" Jamie asked, sounding sulky as he dried his hands with the rooster towel. "For finding her when she got lost?"

"Your grandmother wasn't lost." Abigail gave the lima beans a stir, the pools of delicious bacon fat curling around her wooden spoon. "She…went for a walk and…didn't tell us where she was going."

"Liz Fisher, she's in my class, she told me she saw you and Teacher coming from school Sunday with *Grossmami* in the back of the wagon. Her *mam* told her that—"

"Liz Fisher needs to mind her own knitting," Abigail interrupted. She tapped her left cheekbone. "You missed a spot. Right here."

He took the towel and swiped at his face.

"Don't—" But it was too late. Before she could get the words out, he'd already wiped the kitchen towel on his dirty face. "That was clean," she told him. "Put it in the laundry now."

He groaned, dragging his feet as he walked out of the kitchen.

Abigail grabbed a clean towel from the basket on top of the pie safe. It was probably just as well she didn't have her mother's red rooster towel out. What would Ethan think of an Amish kitchen with a red towel?

Boots began to bark from the porch and Abigail whipped around. She hadn't heard buggy wheels. Ethan must have walked. She turned down the burner under the lima beans and ducked into the bathroom down the hall to catch a quick look at herself in the mirror. Tucking a stray tendril of blond hair into her prayer *kapp*, she walked calmly back through the kitchen and out onto the back porch to greet her guest.

Her *parents'* guest, she reminded herself. He wasn't there to see her.

Or was he?

Supper went even better than Abigail had hoped. Ethan ate heartily, complimenting her on the meal, which made her pleasantly uncomfortable. He and her father seemed to get along well. They talked about crops, about the buggy Ethan and his father were making, and the weather. With spring coming late and too much rain, then not enough, the farmers were all worried about planting. It was the same conversation men had every year, had been having since she was a girl.

Ethan had taken one of her mother's corn muffins, despite Abigail's attempt to keep the basket away from him, but if he noticed how heavily they had been salted or how burnt they were, he didn't show it. He ate the whole thing slathered with fresh-churned butter and blackberry jam and told her mother how good they were. June had giggled with glee, promising to pack a sack of them for him to take home. After supper, it was Abigail's mother who reminded her daughter and Ethan that they should go for a walk.

Abigail was pleasantly surprised that her mother had remembered saying that almost a week ago but embarrassed at the same time that she would bring it up. "*Mam*, I'm sure Ethan needs to get home. I imagine he has chores to do," she said, getting up from her chair. She'd relaxed during the meal and enjoyed herself thoroughly. It was so nice to have someone else at their supper table, to have a younger man again. But suddenly she was anxious. It was kind of Ethan to accept her mother's invitation to supper, but she certainly didn't want him to feel obligated to anything else. Certainly not to *go for a walk* with her.

"Ya," Ethan agreed, still sitting at the foot of the table across from Abigail's father. "I should get home. My *dat*'s hip's acting up. He might need a hand with evening chores." He glanced at Abigail. "Want to walk me to the end of the driveway, Abby?"

Abigail froze, the serving dish of the leftover lima beans in her hands. "I… I best help *Mam* clean up."

"Oh, fiddle!" her mother declared sounding more like her old self than Abigail had heard in months. "Leave the dishes and walk to the end of the lane with *Tietscher.* Your father can help me, and Jamie can, too."

"I have chores," Jamie said sullenly. He'd been quiet throughout the meal, picking at his food, which was unusual. He normally had a big appetite for a boy his size.

"You do have chores," Abigail's father agreed, getting up as he reached for the basket of salty corn muffins. "But they'll wait. You can help your *grossmami* clear off the table, first."

"Women's work," Jamie muttered, staring at his plate.

"Jamie," Abigail scolded. "Don't speak to your grandfather that way."

"Women's work you say?" Ethan asked, his tone easygoing. He picked up his plate and utensils and carried them to the sink. "In my father's house, and it's a big household, we all pitch in together. It's the way my *mam* brought us up. My brothers and I aren't above mopping a kitchen floor or weeding in the garden and my sisters work at the harness shop. They even repair harnesses sometimes."

"They do?" Jamie asked, begrudgingly interested. "How do they know how to do that stuff?"

"My *dat* taught them. My brothers and I taught them." Ethan walked back to the table and grabbed two empty buttermilk glasses. "If you like, you can come home with me one day after school and I'll show you around the shop. Show you what we do."

Jamie looked to his mother as he slid out of his chair. She nodded, silently agreeing she'd let him go. He picked up his plate and silverware and took it to his grandmother.

Abigail's mother took the glasses from Ethan's hands and looked up at him. He towered over her, but she didn't seem to be intimidated. "It was good to have you for supper, Ethan. You come again. Now shoo." She made a sweeping motion with her tiny hands, sudsy from dishwater.

Ethan glanced at Abigail, a look of amusement on his face. "I think we've been dismissed," he told her.

"I think *you* have." She smiled to herself. She liked his sense of humor. It was hard to believe this was the same man she had argued with on more than one occasion. Like on Sunday, tonight he had seemed so relaxed. So easygoing. Not so sad.

Ethan said his goodbyes and left the kitchen. Abigail followed. In the laundry room, he grabbed his straw hat and put it on his head. Abigail donned a sweater that fell open across the front and had no buttons. She'd stitched it herself from navy blue sweatshirt material. It got chilly this time of day, once the sun began to set, and there had been the smell of rain when she'd tossed the potato peels to the chickens earlier.

They were just about to go out the door when Abigail's mother came hurrying after them, a small cloth sack in her hand. "You forgot your corn muffins." Grinning, she held them up to Ethan.

"I sure did. And wouldn't I have been sorry when I'd gotten home and realized I didn't have them," he said, taking the bag from her. "Good night."

Abigail's mother trotted back into the kitchen and Abigail and Ethan took their leave. They walked through the barnyard and headed down the lane, side by side. Boots trailed behind them.

"The meal was great, Abby. Thank you," Ethan said when they were away from the house.

She clasped her hands together looking down as she walked. "You're welcome. It was nice to have someone else at the table. Even though our family is small, back home in Wisconsin we always had friends and neighbors joining us. It was nothing to cook supper for a dozen."

"Well, I enjoyed *not* eating with a dozen people." He glanced at her. "And Rosemary and the girls are good cooks but, phew—" he made a sound of approval "—that *schnitz un kneff*, I'd have to say it's the best I've ever had."

She pressed her lips together to keep from smiling. "You even enjoyed the corn muffins?"

"Probably the best part of the meal," he teased, holding up the cotton sack.

She tried to suppress a chuckle. "You like them that salty?"

He nodded, chuckling with her. "I like them with lots of jam. Lots. And two glasses of water."

She laughed. "That's good because it looks like *Mam* gave you enough to take in your lunch for days." Then looking up at him, she said, "I'm sorry. I didn't mean to trick you. *Mam* made them and she was so proud of them. I tried to warn you at the table not to take one, but I couldn't catch your eye."

"It's fine." He gave a wave of dismissal and met her gaze. "I'd have eaten two more if it would have made your mother happy."

His words touched her and she looked away, surprised by the tightness in her chest. The tenderness she felt for him. He had been so kind to her mother, so friendly with her father and he'd even drawn Jamie into a conversation. Ethan had seemed so comfortable at their table, so comfortable that it was as if he belonged there.

Ethan and Abigail walked in silence for a few steps and then, to change the subject, she said, "It sounds like everything is set for the end-of-the-school-year program next week."

"Thanks to your idea. I think we're going to have a good turnout. I hear a few folks from Seven Poplars might be joining us. They've got a matchmaker over there, Sara Yoder, who's got the idea in her head that it might be a nice event for some of her singles she's trying to make matches with."

Abigail was so surprised she stopped short and the border collie nearly ran into her, he was following her so close. "A matchmaker? I didn't know there was such a thing anymore."

He shrugged. "*Ne?* I'm surprised. She's a cousin to Hannah Hartman from Wisconsin. You didn't know her?"

Abigail chuckled and started to walk again. "Wisconsin is a big state. A lot of Amish communities. I don't know her. But now I'm curious to meet her."

"You're in luck because she'll be there." He stopped where the lane met the blacktop and slid his hands into his pockets. "Did you talk to your *dat* about your *mam* seeing a doctor?"

"I did." She exhaled. "He's not happy, but he's agreed to let her go." She looked down. Her father's dog had plopped himself down in the driveway between the two of them and was looking from one to the other as if following the conversation. She smiled and scratched Boots's head. "But he says he'll be no part of it." She hesitated. "If I take her to the neurologist, you'd be willing to…go along?"

"I sure will. Just say the word."

She met his gaze. "I'd like that."

"Done," he agreed. "Come by the harness shop Monday and use the phone. I'll leave the name and number for you and let my sisters know you'll be by."

She clasped her hands. "Thank you."

He backed onto the road. "You're welcome. See you in church on Sunday?"

"See you in church," she echoed, then watched as he turned and headed down the road.

As she watched him go, once again she found herself disappointed that her time with him had come to an end. She was beginning to think he felt the same way. Why else would he have asked her to walk to the end of the lane with him? She wasn't quite sure what was going on between them, but they had fallen into a friendship she certainly hadn't expected when they met. One she cherished. The thought had crossed her mind more than once in the last two weeks or so that maybe she had feelings for Ethan.

And suddenly, all at once, she realized she did. The question was, what was she going to do with them?

On Fridays, Abigail's mother sometimes liked to take butter, eggs, baked goods and seasonal produce to Spence's Bazaar in Dover where they rented a table and sold the items to the English. It surprised Abigail that her mother would want to go to such a public place when she shied from quilting circles and visits with other women in Hickory Grove. It was Abigail's *dat*'s theory that his wife's excuse in going was to make a little money, but the *real* reason she liked going was to buy things. They would go early so that they could set up their stand before the first shoppers of the day arrived, then Abigail's mother would leave her husband to watch the stand while she prowled through the aisles of antiques and yard sale junk Englishers were selling.

June King loved Spence's. She liked to watch the English tourists in their strange clothing, and she loved to poke through the dusty tables of ceramic knickknacks, kitchen utensils and plastic toys in the flea market. This day, June had, in her eyes, made a real find—an old Amish-style rag doll without a face.

"This is it," June declared, holding up the ragged doll to show her daughter.

Abigail had, at her father's request, trailed her mother at a safe distance, giving her a chance to feel independent without risking her wandering off again. Jamie, who was now on summer vacation from school, had come with them and had agreed to stay with his grandfather and help with the sales.

"She's perfect," Abigail's mother declared, peering into the face of the doll that had no features. "I'm going to buy her and take her home."

"Mam," Abigail said softly. "Jamie doesn't really care for dolls."

Her mother looked at her indignantly. "It's not for *Jamie*." She hugged the doll to her chest. "She's for me. Her name is Annie."

Abigail glanced around. No one seemed to be paying them any mind, not even the two young Mennonite women selling the hand stitched items, both old and new. They also sold embroidery thread and fabric. *"Mam*, are you sure—"

"I'm buying it with my own money," her mother interrupted as she pulled a big white hanky from inside her sleeve where she always kept it. She wrapped it around the doll as if it were a blanket. "She'll have to have some proper clothes. And a prayer *kapp*," she said, walking up to one of the young women. Both Mennonite ladies wore dresses very similar in style to Amish ones, only they were made of calico with a tiny flowered print on the fabric. And instead of a full prayer *kapp*, a piece of round lace rested on top of their hair that they wore in a neat bun at the nape of their necks, similar to Abigail's.

"How much?" Abigail's mother asked.

The young lady responded. Abigail's mother countered the offer and walked away with two dollars saved and two free pieces of fabric big enough to stitch an Amish dress and apron for the doll.

As they walked away from the Mennonites' booth, back toward their own, Abigail shook her head in awe of her mother. Abby had used Millers' harness shop telephone and made an appointment for her mother with the neurologist Rosemary had recommended, but she was wondering if that had been a mistake. Her mother had just been as sharp as a tack, negotiating down the price of the doll. Maybe her father was right. Maybe her mother wasn't slipping into dementia. Maybe she was just stepping further from the confines of Amish rules and customs. She wasn't necessarily breaking them, but like a teenager or young adult preparing to be baptized, she was definitely bending the rules. This had become her father's new theory since the incident where June had wandered off the Miller farm to go swing in the schoolyard.

"Daniel, look what I bought," Abigail's mother called to her husband as they approached him. He was busy taking money from an Englisher woman with hair dyed purple who was buying butter and a bag of chocolate-chip-and-almond cookies Abigail had made. The woman was carrying a cloth bag on her elbow that looked like a handbag. A tiny white dog poked its head out of a hole in the top of the bag.

"Daniel," her mother repeated when he didn't immediately respond.

"Just a minute, June." He gave the purple-haired woman her change and she walked away. "Now let me see."

While her mother showed off her purchase, Abigail glanced around. Spence's seemed busier than any grocery store in town, except maybe the Walmart. Both Amish and Englishers frequented the market on Tuesdays, Fridays and Saturdays, the only days they were open. There were so many things to see and buy and the smells coming from the food area inside the building were enticing. There were homemade baked goods and steak sandwiches, fresh doughnuts and soft pretzels and she could smell the sweet, distinct scent of funnel cakes. The aroma of the funnel cakes made her think of Ethan and his love of sweets. She imagined he liked funnel cake.

It was past lunchtime and her stomach had begun to gurgle. She wondered if it might be a good time to grab something to eat and then pack up what hadn't been sold, though it didn't appear that there would be much to take home. The woman with the purple hair had just bought the last pound of homemade butter they'd wrapped in cheesecloth. There was only a dozen or so cookies left and a couple of bundles of new radishes her father had grown in their hothouse.

Abigail gazed up at the sky. It was clouding up in the west, and it looked as if they might get an afternoon thunderstorm. Better today than tomorrow, she thought to herself. The following day, the end-of-the-year school program and fund-raiser was being held and it would be a shame to get rained out. In the event of bad weather, Ethan had told all of the families they would still hold the spelling bee and the cake auction, but if it rained, it wouldn't be the same because they wouldn't be able to play games and sit outside on blankets and share their picnic suppers.

Abigail turned to her parents. "Anyone hungry? I was thinking about getting a sandwich at the deli." The deli was run by an Amish family that came all the way down from Lancaster and had a reputation for making excellent sandwiches. Her favorite was something they called a Rachel that had pastrami and Swiss cheese and coleslaw on it, of all things on rye bread. And they grilled it on a little griddle that squished the sandwich as it toasted the bread and melted the cheese. "By the time we get home, it will be too late to make dinner. If we're having peas and dumplings for supper," she said, "by the time we get the buggy unpacked and things *ret* up, it will be time to start supper."

"Good idea," her father said. "You know what I like. Italian submarine with pickles and hot peppers."

She nodded. He always got the same thing. *"Mam?"* she asked.

Her mother was sitting on an upturned wooden crate fussing with the doll she had just bought. "If you had a baby, a little girl, I could give her Annie," she said.

Abigail glanced at her father, then back at her mother. She knew her mother meant no offense but the mention of her having another child brought up emotions she tried to keep at bay. Because she did want more babies. She just didn't know if that was in God's plan. *"Mam,* I'm widowed. I...I can't have a baby."

"Grilled cheese," her mother responded. "Pickles on the side. Sweet not sour."

"Hot dog!" Jamie sang. He'd been in a good mood all day, mostly because school was over. Although Abigail had reminded him at the breakfast table that morning that his teacher would still be tutoring him twice a week. The tutoring was coming along well and while Jamie certainly wasn't angelic, she felt as if his behavior was improving. "And potato chips."

Abigail eyed her son. "I don't know that you need chips," she said, though she actually liked them, too. They were homemade and had a better crunch than the kind you bought in a bag at the store. "Want to come with me?"

"*Ne. Grossdadi* and I are playing checkers when we don't have customers." He pointed to the old board her father had had for as long as she could remember.

"Guess I can get them to go instead of on plates." Abigail turned to head in the direction of the deli when her mother popped up off the crate.

"I'll go." She set the doll on the crate and trotted after her daughter.

The line to place orders was long at the deli, but Abigail didn't mind. She actually ended up standing behind Eunice Gruber and her daughter May who looked to be about fourteen or fifteen. They were in the same church district. Despite the warnings she'd gotten from several people that Eunice could be a bit of a gossip, Abigail had liked the woman at once. She was friendly and she was always nothing but kind and patient with Abigail's mother.

"Nice to see you," Eunice greeted as Abigail and her mother got into line.

"Nice to see you. It's busy here today," Abigail commented, nodding in the direction of the deli counter. They must have had half a dozen Amish women working. One took orders, one ran the cash register at the other end of the counter, and four ladies were busy cutting meat and cheese for those who were ordering by the pound or making sandwiches.

"Always like this on Fridays," Eunice said. "But the line moves pretty fast." She nodded to Abigail's mother. "Good to see you out, June. We missed you at the quilting circle this week."

"Not much for quilting," June answered. "Busy. Very busy."

"You just never know who you'll run into at Spence's, do you?" a man said from behind Abigail.

She knew the deep voice and she immediately felt her cheeks grow warm. She spun around to see Ethan with his brother Jacob getting into line behind them. Though Joshua and Jacob were identical twins, Phoebe had pointed out a spattering of freckles across Jacob's nose that Joshua didn't have, so now Abigail could tell the difference between them.

She couldn't resist a big smile. "Never know, do you?"

Ethan met her gaze and she felt a little tingle of… something, something warm and pleasant and…his smile just made her feel good. And the way he looked at her, she realized that he felt it, too.

"Getting sandwiches for the crew." He hooked his thumb in the direction of where dozens of buggies were hitched in a parking lot. "Our little brother James decided to throw a fit when Rosemary told him no ice cream. Then Josiah joined in, so she took them both to the buggy. Almost nap time, I think."

"They're not even two yet." Abigail gave a wave of dismissal. "They've probably had a busy morning."

"Busy morning," Abigail mother repeated loudly to Eunice.

"Good afternoon, June." Ethan pressed his hand to his flat stomach. "I think I'm still full of that supper you cooked up last week."

"Busy, busy, busy," Abigail's mother went on to Eunice, paying no mind to Ethan. "We're planning a wedding, you know."

Abigail froze. Her eyes widened.

Eunice drew back in obvious delight. "I didn't. You hadn't mentioned you had another daughter or is it a son?"

"My little Babby. Abigail," her mother said proudly, standing a little straighter. "Getting married. To the schoolmaster." She grinned and pointed right at Ethan.

Abigail's face flamed so hot, she was sure she was the color of her mother's rooster dish towel. She was so mortified that she didn't know what to say. Even with all the people in line and milling around in the deli with all the noise, there was no way Ethan hadn't heard her.

"Mam," Abigail said quietly, tugging on her mother's sleeve. "No one's getting married," she whispered into her ear. *"I'm* not getting married."

"He's a very nice young man," Abigail's mother went on, paying no mind to her daughter. "He'll make a good husband, a good father to my grandson and the little ones to follow."

Eunice's face had lit up. She looked Ethan's way, then back at Abigail's mother. "He certainly will, and to think everyone in Hickory Grove thought he'd stay a bachelor. Most eligible bachelor in the county some would say."

"Such a busy time," Abigail's mother went on. "We have so much to do, guests to invite…"

Her mother's voice faded in her head as Abigail turned to Ethan. "I'm so sorry," she whispered, so humiliated that she couldn't meet his gaze.

"Abby," he said gently.

"I have no idea where she got such a—"

"Abby," Ethan interrupted, keeping his voice down.

Jacob was looking up, pretending to be entranced by the menu posted on a big white board hanging by chains over the deli counter.

"It's fine," Ethan went on.

She covered her face with her hands. "I don't know

what to—" She exhaled. "I'm just glad we have that appointment with the doctor coming up." She dropped her hands, looking up at Ethan, knowing her cheeks had to be bright red. "Thank you for being so nice about this. It's embarrassing for me and for you."

"Embarrassing?" Ethan knit his brows. "Are you kidding? These ladies just made my day. Apparently, I'm the most eligible Amish bachelor in Kent County." He leaned forward. "And speaking of such things, I heard some guys talking about you at the mill the other day."

"Me?" She drew back.

He shrugged. "You're single, too. A pretty, smart woman like yourself, it will only be a matter of time before someone asks to court you." He held her gaze. "Almost makes me think I ought to—" He cut himself off from what he was saying and pointed ahead. "I think you're next in line."

She hesitated. He'd been about to say something, but what? She thought to press him, but then her mother took off for the deli counter and she had to hurry after her. "See you tomorrow," she called to Ethan.

"See you tomorrow," he answered. "Hey, Abby, what kind of cake are you making?"

"Lemon icebox," she responded. She didn't look back, but she could feel him watching her. Had he been about to ask if he could court her? Her heart gave a little pitter pat and she suddenly felt ten years younger.

Chapter Ten

At noon on the day of the school program, Ethan loaded his wagon in the barnyard with a couple of tables he was borrowing from his district's church wagon. His prayers had been answered and it was a bright and sunny cloudless day with the temperature reaching seventy-eight degrees. Most folks attending the program would bring blankets to sit on in the grass to eat, but in anticipation that a few of the elderly might prefer to sit in a chair at a table, he'd decided to haul some over to the school. He also needed a table to display the cakes that would be auctioned off. With the money he was hoping they would raise, he intended to buy some new books for the classroom and maybe even one of those fancy whiteboards to replace the chalkboard that had to be fifty years old if it was a day. The thing was so old and had been cleaned so many times that fresh chalk barely showed on it.

As Ethan started adding chairs to the wagon, his father came walking up from the milk house.

Benjamin's hip had improved with the warmer weather and today he was barely limping. "Good day for a picnic," he greeted. "Rosemary's girls are all aflutter. Looks like a bakery in our kitchen right now. I hear Ginger is sweet on someone and hoping he'll bid on her cake."

Ethan chuckled. "Ginger is always sweet on someone and there's an endless line of boys wanting to take her home from a singing. Be interesting to see who she ends up with when she's ready to get serious about courting." He walked back to the church wagon. "You're right. Couldn't have asked for a better day. Warm enough so folks won't get chilled, but cool enough that the cakes the women are baking won't melt."

His father had a piece of straw in his mouth and he was chewing on it thoughtfully. He halted between the church wagon and Ethan's. "You plan to bid on a cake?" It was a tradition at this type of affair that husbands always bid on wives' cakes, but single men tended to bid on cakes baked by women they were sweet on.

Ethan grabbed another wooden folding chair and added it to the ones he was taking to the school. Once they were all loaded, he'd secure them with straps so they wouldn't bang around or tumble out on the ride. "I imagine I ought to. Me being the schoolmaster and the one running this shindig today."

His father eyed him. "Anyone's cake in particular you fancy?"

Ethan took another chair from the church wagon but lowered it to the gravel driveway, contemplating what to say. He'd been thinking about that very question since the day before when he'd bumped into Abby at Spence's. He wanted to bid on her cake. He wanted to sit on a blanket and share a picnic supper with her and talk with her and laugh with her, but he didn't know if that was the right thing to do. The idea of it all was so overwhelming that it had kept him up half the night.

It seemed as if in the last few weeks, his minutes, hours, days were strung together by the time he spent with her. The time he waited to see her again. The last weeks of school, they had ended up walking to her place every afternoon and those times with her had been the best of his day. She was so easy to talk to, whether it was about something as simple as a science lesson he'd taught on the life cycle of a frog, or the more serious topic of being widowed. It seemed like his Mary and her Egan came up in conversation all the time and he was astonished by how easy it was to talk to her about his wife. How easy it was to hear about her husband. Abby understood him, understood his pain in a way no one else he knew understood, not even his *dat* and Rosemary who had lost their spouses, too.

Ethan had been denying it for weeks, but the truth was, somehow on those afternoon walks, at her father's supper table, at the noonday meal at church, standing in line at Spence's, he'd fallen in love with Abby. But how could that be possible? He still loved Mary.

Ethan looked up to see his father watching him intently.

"You going to bid on Abigail's cake?" Benjamin asked. Not much got by his father.

Ethan picked up the chair and carried it to the wagon. "Thinking about it."

"What's to think about?" His father chewed on the bit of straw, fiddling with the end of it with his fingers. "Nice girl. Strong in her faith. Can cook. From what I hear, she can run a farm on her own." He narrowed his gaze. "Why *wouldn't* you bid on her cake?"

When Ethan didn't answer, his father went on. "Why wouldn't you want to snatch her up before someone else does? You know, Eli was asking me about her yesterday. I think he has half a mind to call on her. Next thing you know, we'll be attending their wedding."

Eli Kutz lived down the road a piece and was a widower with four children. He wanted badly to remarry, not just to provide a mother for his children, but because he had told Ethan that he felt like only half a man without a woman at his side. He'd been interested in Phoebe back when she was single, but in the end, it had been Joshua she had married. Ethan had felt bad for Eli, but at the same time, he'd known Phoebe wasn't the woman for him.

"Don't you like her?" Ethan's father pressed. "You seem like you like her. Seems like she likes you. The two of you have your heads together every time I see you."

"I do like her." Ethan took his time arranging the chair just so, stalling as he searched for the right words. He wasn't like his *dat* or his brother Joshua. Talking about how he felt came hard. At least with most people. It was Abby who could get him to talk. To say things he'd never said to anyone else. "It's just that I…" He exhaled and didn't go on.

"You just what, *sohn*?"

Ethan turned to his father, taking off his hat and wiping his forehead. "I…I feel like I'm betraying Mary somehow." His voice caught in his throat and it was a moment before he could go on. He took his time pulling his hat back on his head just so. "I have feelings for Abby, but how can that be possible?" He lifted his gaze to his father and was surprised to see tears in the older man's eyes. "I loved her so much, *Dat*."

His father plucked the straw from his mouth and tossed it on the driveway. He rubbed his eldest son's back as if Ethan was one of his toddlers. "Of course you loved her. She was your wife. But she's gone, Ethan." He looked up, seeming unashamed of his tears. "You don't think I loved your mother? Still love her? But I love Rosemary, too. It's different. She's a different woman than your mother was. I'm a different man than I was when your mother and I married." He shrugged. "I don't think we can only love one person, *sohn*."

Ethan looked away, afraid he was going to tear up.

"I don't think God means for His people to be that way." His father was quiet for a moment and then went on. "You know, after you were born and we were expecting your sister Mary, I worried that I loved you so much, how would I love the next babe? And the next who came along and the next? But I did. And then to have Josiah and James come along at a point in mine and Rosemary's life when we thought there would be no more children?" He gestured in the direction of the farmhouse with a meaty hand. "I love them every bit as much as I love you, as I love your brothers, and your sister. See…God's love isn't limited, and we're made in his image, Ethan. You understand what I'm saying?"

Ethan was quiet for a long moment and then said as much to himself as to his father, "I think I do love Abby. Like you said," he went on, thinking out loud. "It's different, but—I'm falling in love with her. I've fallen in love with her."

His father grinned as he took his hanky from his

pocket and wiped his eyes. "Then I think you best bid on her cake and marry her before Eli beats you to her."

"Marry her?" Ethan drew back. "We haven't even courted."

"What do you think you been doing all these weeks? It's not as if you're kids. You couldn't take her to a taffy pull or drive her home from a singing the way we did in our youth. Those walks you two been taking? That's been your courting time, you've just been too stubborn to see it. Don't you remember how I courted Rosemary? At her supper table. With her at ours. Under the trees after Sunday service when we talked."

Everything his father was saying made so much sense that Ethan almost felt like a dunce. He prided himself, maybe sometimes too much, in being a smart man. He certainly hadn't been smart with Abby. It had been there right in front of his eyes all this time. *She* had been right there.

His father walked over to the church wagon, picked up a chair and carried it to his son. He pushed it into Ethan's hands. "You know nothing would make me happier than to see you bring Abigail and her boy here to be a part of our family. Nothing would give me greater pleasure than to see you raise your own little ones right here on this farm." He adjusted the brim on his straw hat. "So what do you have to say, *sohn*?"

His father's smile was infectious. "I think I'll be bidding on an icebox lemon cake."

Abigail was delighted that Saturday was a perfect day for Ethan's school event; the sun was shining, and there was a slight breeze to keep everyone from getting overly warm. All of the parents, relatives and friends who lived in the community turned out, as well as Sara Yoder, the matchmaker from Seven Poplars. With her, she brought two wagons and a buggy of single young men and women.

The spelling bee had been a great hit with the parents and students alike, and the Fishers' oldest daughter still in school, Miriam, had won the grand prize. The school board had awarded her a gift certificate to Walmart by spelling the word *koinonia*, which meant Christian fellowship, taken from the Book of Acts in the Bible.

After the spelling bee, several students gave presentations and then there was a volleyball game between the girls and boys. The bonnets won, hands down because Bishop Simon decreed that all the straw hats would have a handicap. The boys had their ankles tied together with lengths of corn string so that they were hobbled. It made for many tumbles and even more laughter. After that came an egg and spoon race, adult men against their wives, and the men had been forced to use raw eggs. The losing team, consisting of fathers and grandfathers, would have to clean up afterward.

Eli Kutz brought his red cart and driving goats so that all the small children got rides. There was hymn singing by grades one through three, and a greased pig competition for boys between the ages of four and ten. After a hilarious contest and many near misses, one of the Gruber children caught the pig and got to keep it, much to the delight of his mother.

"Roast suckling pig for Christmas dinner," Eunice cried, clapping her hands. But everyone knew that they wouldn't really eat his pig. Ethan's brother-in-law, Marshall, who had donated the piglet, had promised to trade the greased pig, a male, for a young sow. The boy would use that pig to start his own breeding project. If he was diligent, he'd have the start of his own herd and be earning money from the animals by the time he was a teenager.

Throughout the afternoon, Abigail kept her *mam* at her side as she helped organize the games and prepare for the cake auction. Abigail hadn't taken part in the volleyball because she didn't want to be anywhere near Ethan. She'd taken enough teasing from Phoebe who had heard from Eunice that June had announced that Abigail and the teacher were getting married. It wasn't that Abigail didn't want to talk to Ethan or that she was upset with him; she was just biding her time until she could talk to him alone. She was hoping he would bid on her cake. She thought he would. Otherwise, why else would he have asked her what she was making for the auction?

Once the games had concluded and the women began unloading their picnic baskets, the auction began. It was Benjamin who had volunteered to serve as the auctioneer. He held a three-layer cake high in the air. "So first we have a chocolate-on-chocolate cake with more chocolate, baked by—" He halted and leaned over to whisper to the matchmaker from Seven Poplars who was standing beside him. Abigail had been introduced to her but had barely had time to say more than hello when she was called to settle a spat between Jamie and one of his classmates. Sara, a plump, dark-skinned woman with a bright smile, whispered back to Ethan's father. "Baked by Amanda Beiler, visiting us from Arkansas. What are we bid?" Benjamin called in his deep auctioneer's voice. Though the names of the bakers were announced, bidders had to be ready to act fast because no one knew in which order they'd be auctioned off.

"One dollar!" a young man in a blue shirt who Abigail didn't recognize called out.

"None of that," Benjamin flung back. "This is for the school. These boys and girls need one of those fancy chalkboards that you don't even need chalk for. I hear you use some kind of markers. Come on, son, we know you can dig deeper into your pockets. We're starting this bidding at five dollars!"

Six came and then seven. There was laughter and teasing and the boy in the blue shirt bid nine dollars for the chocolate cake. Samuel brought a rubber mallet down on the table and handed Amanda Beiler's supper basket to the blushing boy. Amanda took the cake and the two went off amid whistles and hoots to find a place to spread their tablecloth in the shade.

One after another, the cakes were sold. They fairly flew off the table as money jingled and rustled into a big pottery cookie jar on the auction table. One of the Fisher girls' pineapple upside down cakes sold for twelve dollars, and then Joshua bought Phoebe's pudding dish cake for fourteen dollars. After that, Bishop Simon offered to stand in as auctioneer and got a roar of approval when Benjamin successfully bid on both Rosemary's cream sponge cake and his youngest stepdaughter Tara's jelly roll, paying thirty dollars for the two of them.

Abigail's father bid on his wife's Bundt cake that hadn't risen, paying twenty-one dollars for it, then another four cakes went to single boys the matchmaker had brought along. After that, Abigail lost count of the cakes and the money being raised for the school until the bishop raised her lemon icebox cake high.

"Ten dollars!" Eli Kutz shouted before the bishop had opened his mouth.

Abigail and several others turned to look at the widower who was stepping to the front of the crowd.

"Looks delicious," the bishop said. "So delicious I might bid on it myself if I wouldn't think I'd be in hot water with my wife, Annie."

Everyone laughed.

"So ten dollars," Bishop Simon said. "Who will give me fifteen? Come on, boys. I don't think I've ever seen a lemon icebox cake that looked this good."

Abigail could feel herself blushing. She didn't want to eat her picnic supper with Eli, though he was a nice enough man. She wanted Ethan to bid on it, but what if, being the schoolmaster, he wasn't supposed to bid? What if he didn't want to? She suddenly wished she hadn't made the cake. If Eli won, she'd have to have supper with him and his children. Not that it would be so terrible, but—

"Fifty dollars," came a deep voice from beside the auction table.

Everyone gasped. Abigail knew that voice. It was Ethan's, and she couldn't help but break into an embarrassed grin.

"Fifty dollars?" the bishop gasped. "I'd say that young man likes icebox cakes, wouldn't you?"

Everyone clapped and the bishop brought the rubber mallet down hard on the table. "Sorry, Eli. Sold for fifty dollars to the schoolmaster who's given us all a fine afternoon. Seems like we ought to be paying him, though, eh?"

There was more clapping as Ethan walked up to the table and pushed a handful of bills into the cookie jar. The next thing Abigail knew, she was walking beside him.

"How about over there under that oak tree?" Ethan asked her quietly. No one was paying much attention to them as the last couple of cakes were auctioned off and everyone was finding a place to set out their picnic suppers.

Abigail nodded, not being able to find her voice quite yet. Ethan had bid on her cake! He had paid fifty dollars for it, an astronomical price for a cake, even at a fund-raiser. To pay that much was almost a declaration that they were a couple. The idea made her nervous and excited at the same time as she wondered if he would bring up the subject or if she would be forced to.

"This basket feels heavy enough to be packed with rocks." Ethan looked down at her. "You brought lots of food. Good. I could eat a horse I'm so hungry."

"Not Butterscotch, I hope," she answered as she followed him, keeping her eyes on his back, trying not to make eye contact with their neighbors. Eunice Gruber, in particular, seemed to be interested and watched them go by without even pretending not to be staring.

"Not Butterscotch the horse, but maybe some butterscotch pudding," Ethan told her. "You bring some of that?"

"What? Cake isn't enough dessert?" she teased. "Sorry, no butterscotch pudding, but I did bring fried chicken, coleslaw, and macaroni salad, sweet pickles, corn bread and honey butter."

"All my favorite foods. How's this?" Ethan asked when they reached the oak tree.

"Good." She set the cake down on level ground and

glanced up to see Jamie settling down with her folks on an old blue quilt her *mam* had made many years ago. From there she could keep an eye on him. She was annoyed that he'd caused trouble earlier and didn't want him getting into any more altercations.

Ethan waited for her to take out the checked yellow tablecloth she'd brought and spread it on the ground. Most people were already eating.

Abigail knelt and began removing the fried chicken and macaroni salad from the picnic basket.

"You know I'd have bid a hundred dollars to beat Eli out of that cake," Ethan said to her.

Abigail met his gaze and knew that she'd not imagined her feelings for him. Or his for her. Suddenly she felt shy and she busied herself preparing the feast. He sat, stretching long legs out while she still knelt. "You didn't have to buy my cake for that much money," she said. She unfolded foil-wrapped chicken and passed Ethan a plate and several paper napkins.

"Sure I did. Otherwise, Eli would be having supper with you and I wouldn't." He sprinkled salt and pepper on a chicken leg and looked up at her. "Can I drive you home after supper?"

Abigail served him a large portion of macaroni salad and gave herself a smaller one, then handed him a fork. "We'll have to clean up after supper. Load the tables and such."

"After we clean up? Just the two of us?"

She lifted her gaze to find Ethan studying her intently and she realized something had changed in him. Something had changed between them. "I suppose Jamie could just go home with *Mam* and *Dat*."

"He could."

Ethan was still smiling two hours later as he eased Butterscotch down the schoolyard lane. Everything had been cleaned up and they were the last folks to leave. "Nice night tonight," he said, the sounds of insects and peepers clicking and croaking all around them. When he reached the blacktop of the road, he reined his horse in. "Feel like taking the long way home?"

"I don't know. I should get home to be sure Jamie's in bed."

"Come on," he cajoled. "Jamie will be fine." He shrugged. "He's already been in trouble today. Bet he's in bed, as well behaved as any nine-year-old boy can be."

She hesitated.

"And I want to talk to you."

She gave a little laugh but inside she was pleased. "Talk to me?" she teased. "We talked for more than an hour over supper. Most everyone else had eaten, packed up and headed home and there the two of us were still talking."

He glanced at her. "Nice wasn't it?"

She nodded.

He must have taken that to mean they could take the long way home because instead of turning right to head for her parents' place, he turned left. For several minutes they rode side by side on the wagon bench in comfortable silence. Of course, the evening wasn't really silent because of the clip-clop of Butterscotch's hooves, the creaking of the wooden wagon wheels as they rolled, and the sounds of the insects, critters and creatures that came out after the sunset.

"So what I wanted to talk to you about." Ethan cleared his throat. "I've been trying to think all afternoon how to say this, Abby, and I can't think of any way to do it but to just come out and say it."

She looked at him and was about to speak when he blurted, "I think I'm falling in love with you."

Her breath caught in her throat.

"Ne," he said, gripping the reins tightly in his hands and pulling the wagon to stop right there in the middle of the road. "I *have* fallen in love with you. I… I'm in love with you, Abby, and I think—" For a moment he just held her gaze and then smiled. "I guess I've known it for weeks, I just… I didn't understand."

She nodded, knowing exactly what he was talking about. "You didn't understand how you could care for another woman when you loved Mary. When you still do." She nibbled on her lower lip, amazed she could speak so freely with him.

The sound of a car and a flash of headlights came from behind them and Ethan made a clicking sound between his teeth to urge Butterscotch forward again. Even with the electric lights on the back of the wagon, run by a battery under the seat, it wasn't safe to sit on the road. He waited until a blue sedan passed them and glanced at Abigail again. "It was my *dat* who set me straight. You know Rosemary isn't my *mam.* My *mam* died. And Rosemary's husband died. The way *Dat* explained it to me was that a man can love more than one woman, a woman can love more than one man in a lifetime. He said God made us in his image and He can love many."

She wiped at her eyes that had gone misty. When he explained it like that, it made so much more sense to her. Made her feel so much better because somewhere in the back of her head she had been thinking she was somehow betraying Egan by caring for Ethan, but suddenly she knew it wasn't true.

They rode in silence for a few minutes before Ethan spoke up again. "I'm sorry if this is too much. Too soon, Abby. I know we haven't known each other but what, two or three months?"

"Well, three months ago we'd just arrived in Hickory Grove and you were telling me what a naughty boy my son was," she said with amusement.

"And you weren't having any of it, were you?"

"The first couple of times, I had patience with you, but that last time. The outhouse incident…"

"Phew," he said. "I don't think I've ever had a parent quite so angry with me."

"I wasn't angry."

He cut his eyes at her.

"Okay," she confessed, "I *was* angry, but I'm not anymore. You were right but none of that matters because—" She took a deep breath, feeling the way she had the first time she'd ever run off the dock at home back in Wisconsin, held her breath and jumped into their pond. It was a light-headedness that was scary and exhilarating at the same time. "It doesn't matter, Ethan, because… because I love you, too."

"You do?"

"Ya," she said bashfully.

He slid his hand across the wooden bench and covered her hand with his. "Tell me something about Egan."

"What?"

"I want to hear more about Egan."

"Like what?" she asked.

"Anything you want to tell. The way I see it, the

more I know about him, the more I'll know about you.
I guess I want to know everything."

His words touched a place in her heart that she didn't
know could ever be touched again and she began to
talk. By the time they were back on her parents' road,
the subject had changed to talk of his Mary. He told
her about the log cabin quilts she used to make, that
she added honey to her applesauce instead of sugar and
how she'd always been one for losing things. And with
each thing he told, Abigail felt strangely closer to him.

By the time they drove up her father's lane, Ethan
was holding her hand. There were rules about unmarried men and women touching, but Abigail didn't care.
It just felt right.

In the barnyard, Ethan climbed down from the
wagon and walked around to help Abigail down. The
only light on in the house was the glow of a lamp from
her parents' upstairs bedroom. As he walked her toward
the house, he kept hold of her hand.

Abigail felt as if she was floating. It had been a long
time since she had remembered being this happy. "So,"
she said stopping just beside the porch. All the openness
between them had suddenly made her bold. "What are
we going to do about this?"

"This?" he asked.

"Us," she said.

He took her other hand and stood facing her. They
were both smiling, and she knew, just *knew*, he was
going to ask her to walk out with him.

"What are we going to do?" he repeated. Then he
shrugged. "I guess the only thing to do is for me to ask
you to marry me."

Abigail was so shocked that, for a moment, she

couldn't respond. "M-marry you? Ethan, we haven't even courted yet."

"According to my *dat*, we have been. For weeks, months, by his tally and… Abby, I know you're the right woman for me and I think I'm the right man for you. I haven't been able to talk to someone else like this since Mary—" He stopped midsentence and looked away.

The moment the words came out of his mouth he drew his lip tight as if he wished he hadn't said that. "I'm sorry," he told her. "I shouldn't have said that. Here I am trying to woo you and I'm talking about my dead wife." He closed his eyes for a moment shaking his head. "I'm sorry," he repeated.

"Ne," she whispered, taking her hand from his to brush it against his cheek. Her eyes were welling with tears again. As ridiculous as it seemed, hearing him speak of his wife made her love him more. "Don't ever apologize for speaking her name. Promise me." She gazed into his eyes. "And I'll never hold back from talking about Egan. They're a part of us, Ethan. Don't you see that? Mary is who made you who you are in some ways. She made you the person I love."

"Is that a yes?" Ethan asked. "You'll marry me?"

He was so close at that moment that Abigail thought he might kiss her. It was prohibited of course. They weren't unbaptized teenagers. Kissing was for husbands and wives, but she found herself leaning toward him anyway.

"Ya," I'll marry you," she whispered.

Their lips had almost touched when suddenly Ethan cried out and they were splashed with what seemed like a bucket of cold water.

"Oh!" Abigail cried, stepping away from Ethan to look up in the direction the water had come.

And there, leaning out the window, was Jamie, ready to toss another water balloon.

"Jamie Stolz!" she called up at him.

He disappeared from sight and slammed the window shut.

"I'm so sorry," she said as Ethan removed his hat, dripping with water. Her face was covered in water and so was her dress. And so was Ethan's shirt.

He started to laugh as he wiped his face with a dry spot on his sleeve.

"It's not funny!" she told him, marching toward the back porch.

"It's not, but don't be too hard on him," he called after her as she went up the steps.

He was still laughing when she walked into the house and closed the door.

Chapter Eleven

The garden soil was warm between Abigail's bare toes and she took a moment to appreciate the blessing of the warm day, the final crop of fragrant strawberries she was dropping into her bucket and her betrothal to Ethan.

In some ways, it seemed as if everything had moved so quickly between the two of them. It was mid-June and she and Ethan had already been to see the bishop and set their wedding day for the last Thursday in August so that they could be married before the school year began. At the same time, it seemed as if she had known Ethan a lifetime and their impending marriage was simply the next stepping-stone in their lives. She couldn't wait to be his wife and walk through the life they had been given by God, hand in hand.

Both of their families were thrilled with the match, which made the engagement all the more exciting. Abigail's mother couldn't wait for the wedding and had her husband busy sprucing up the interior of the house with new coats of paint in anticipation of the upcoming ceremony, which would be held in their home.

Abigail glanced across the strawberry patch at Jamie.

He was kneeling, bucket beside him for strawberries, but he wasn't picking. Something had caught his interest in the soil. "Move along," she told her son gently. "The sun's climbing higher in the sky. You'll soon be complaining it's too hot out here and we have the rest of the patch to finish."

"Ants," Jamie said pointing.

"Ah, you found an anthill." She'd seen several that morning; everyone on the farm was busy. She plucked a fat red berry and eased it into her tin bucket so as not to bruise it.

"Did you know that ants are some of the strongest creatures in the world for their size?" Jamie asked still watching the ants. "They can carry up to like three *thousand* times their weight before their heads fall off. And they can even get other ants to help them and carry heavier things."

She nodded, moving up a little and parting the leaves in search of more ripe berries. There were no green ones left. She doubted there would be another picking. The only reason they still had *any* strawberries the third week of June was that spring had come late that year. "You learn that in science class at school?" she asked.

She knew for a fact that ants had been a topic of discussion the final week of school because Ethan had told her how well Jamie had done on his test. Not only had his reading improved, but his writing, as well. He'd gotten an A on the test and Ethan had tacked it to a bulletin board with the other A's in the classes from that week.

Jamie shrugged, losing interest in the ants, and turned back to the strawberry patch. "I guess."

"Ethan said you liked the unit on insects." She placed another strawberry in the pail. "Is that true?"

He lowered his head so that she couldn't see his face

beneath his straw hat. "All you do is talk about him," he grumbled.

"Talk about who?"

"*Ethan*. It's all Ethan this and Ethan that." He took an irritable tone to his voice. "*Ethan's* coming for my reading lesson. We're going to *Ethan's* house for supper. We have to walk with *Ethan* to church on Sunday."

She sat back on her heels. "I thought you liked Ethan. Jamie, he's helped you so much with reading. He says at the rate you're going, you'll be reading at the same level as the other boys in your class by Christmas. He says you're very smart."

Jamie threw a strawberry into the weeds beyond the garden.

"I hope that was a rotten one." Abigail pointed in the direction of the strawberry he'd just tossed. "We don't waste food."

"It was. A bug got it." He batted at the strawberry plants as he searched for another ripe berry, his picking only half-hearted now. "And see what I mean. *Ethan* says I'm smart. Ethan. Ethan. Ethan."

Abigail took a moment to gather her thoughts before she spoke. She had sensed her son wasn't keen on her betrothal, but she had been telling herself he just needed time to adjust to the idea. They hadn't really talked about it. "You know Ethan and I are going to marry in August, and then we'll live around the corner at his place. So you may as well get used to him."

"He's not my *dat*." There was anger in her son's voice now.

"No, he's not," she said gently. "And we'll never ask you to call him that. No one can ever replace your father, but I hope that you'll come to care for him as my husband. And as your stepfather." She hesitated and then went on, though what she was about to say wasn't something an Amish woman usually discussed with her son. "You know, God may bless me with more children. You would be a big brother to them. And Ethan would be their *vadder*, so…he could be as much your *dat* as you want him to be."

Jamie chewed on that for a moment. "I don't want brothers and sisters. And I don't want to move." He met her gaze stubbornly. "I want to stay here."

"But we're going to have a new house." She kept her tone upbeat, trying not to get frustrated with him. She knew this had to be overwhelming for him. "Ethan's already broken ground. It's going to have a big wrap-around porch and—and we'll be close enough for you to walk over to see your grandparents. You can stop every day after school if you like."

It had been decided that Ethan would build them a *grossdadi* house of sorts, one smaller than the big farmhouse where he currently lived with his father and Rosemary and their children. It would be set on a little knoll, through the orchard behind the big house. Eventually, Ethan and Abigail and their children would take the larger farmhouse and Rosemary and Benjamin and whoever was left at home of their children would move into the little house. With their twins being ten years younger than Rosemary's youngest by her previous marriage, it made sense that eventually there would just be the four of them and they would take the smaller house. It was what Benjamin and Rosemary wanted, according to Ethan, and because it was what *he* wanted, it was what Abigail wanted. Besides, it really did make sense.

"I want to stay here with *Grossmami* and *Grossdadi*," Jamie whined. "Can't I stay here with them? You can go live with Ethan at his place."

"You can't stay here," she said gently. "Because I'd miss you too much. And because you're my son and I'm your *mam*. Children live with their parents."

"Then you should stay here, too." He threw another rotten strawberry, harder this time. "I don't see why you even have to get married at all."

She dropped her hands to her lap. Her fingertips were stained red with berry juice as was her apron. "It's what men and women do, *boppli*," she said using a childish endearment. "It's God's wish that when we grow up, we marry. Someday you'll marry and then you'll live with your wife."

"I like it here," he argued. "I don't want to get married. I don't want you to get married. I just want things to stay the same."

She glanced away in frustration. As if she didn't have enough to worry about with her *mam* this week, now Jamie was going to act out? It wasn't that her *mam* had been overly difficult the last few days. Actually, she'd been pretty good. The wedding had given her something to focus on and she'd even been doing a little cooking successfully. But Monday she and Ethan had taken June for her follow-up appointment with the neurologist and the doctor had confirmed that it was likely her *mam* was showing early signs of Alzheimer's. Abigail had tried to listen to the doctor as she gently explained that there was no way to predict how quickly or slowly the disease would progress. It was Ethan who had comforted Abigail on the way home by saying that no matter what happened with her mother later down the road, he would be there to help the family.

Abigail shifted her gaze to her son who was just sitting there now, not even attempting to pick strawberries. She felt bad that Jamie was upset about her impending marriage, but the fact of the matter was that a nine-year-old boy didn't get to play a part in that decision for his mother. And as for not wanting siblings, had Egan lived, she and Egan certainly wouldn't have consulted Jamie before having any more children. It wasn't a child's place.

"Jamie," she said, surprised how strong her voice was. She wasn't being unkind, but she was definitely being firm. "I'm sorry you're not happy about the changes in our lives, but you'll adjust with time. In the meantime, I expect you to be respectful of Ethan and of my decision."

Jamie just sat there.

"Do you understand me, *sohn*?" she said.

When he didn't respond, she repeated herself a little more sharply.

"Ya," Jaimie conceded.

She looked down and parted the strawberry leaves in front of her, in search of another berry. "*Goot.* Now get to work. Finish that section of picking and then you can go play for an hour before you finish the rest of your chores."

And with that, she returned to the task at hand and tried to decide what she would take for dessert to Ethan's house for Friday night supper.

Ethan walked beside Abigail, her hand in his. It felt good. Not all couples held hands before marrying but he had gotten so used to seeing the physical affection between his father and Rosemary, and Phoebe and his brother, that he wanted that kind of warmth in his and Abby's courting and later in their marriage. If that was acceptable to Abigail, of course. It seemed to be.

Ethan and Mary had never been physically affectionate in front of people because that wasn't how she had been raised, but he liked the fact that Abigail was more open to the idea. Maybe because her parents weren't shy about showing their feelings for each other. While Ethan had not tried to kiss Abigail again since the night they'd become engaged and Jamie had dropped the water balloon on them, he had made it a point to hold her hand when they were alone together. They were still talking a lot, getting to know each other, which was bringing them closer together, but for some reason her touch also made him feel closer to her. It seemed to form a connection that lasted long after they had said goodbye.

"I can't believe you got me out of washing dishes again," she chastised gently as they walked through the orchard that he and his father and brothers had expanded that spring.

The summer solstice was almost upon them so the sun was just setting, though it was eight thirty at night. It was a nice evening, warm and humid but not hot. Fireflies flickered between the branches of the trees. There was an orchard on the rear of the large property but this one was only about five years old. He liked the idea that they would have to walk through the field of Liberty and Golden Delicious apple, Clingstone and Lorin peach, and sour cherry trees to go from the big house to their smaller one. It would give them a little privacy, the kind a newly married couple needed. An orchard also made a nice front yard, he had decided.

"Rosemary and your sisters will think I don't know how to *ret* up a kitchen after supper," Abigail went on. She was complaining about not staying back to clean up, but it was only half-hearted. He had a feeling she enjoyed these stolen moments of time alone together as much as he did.

He squeezed her hand. "It was Rosemary who told me to take you out to see the foundation we laid this week. So you've officially been excused from cleanup. And she was going to get June to dry dishes, so you needn't worry about your mother."

"That's so kind of Rosemary," Abigail said, glancing at him. "She's so patient with *Mam*." She smiled up at him. "With me."

Abigail was as pretty as a picture this evening in a rose-colored dress and white apron, her prayer *kapp* string looped and dangling beguilingly at the nape of her neck. Blond tendrils of hair peeked from beneath her *kapp* and made him smile. He was so happy. After being so sad for so long, he just couldn't believe this was all real. That Abigail was real. He wished now that his faith had been stronger, that he had believed God would bring him happiness again. It was a mistake he would learn from. One he believed had made his faith stronger.

"Rosemary likes you," he went on. "And so do the girls," he added, referring to his stepsisters and Joshua's wife, Phoebe, who lived with them, too. Eventually Joshua and Phoebe intended to build on a plot of land at the back of the property near the old orchard, but for now, they were using their money to expand his greenhouse business. "Why wouldn't they?" he asked. "You're smart and kind and you're going to take me off their hands." He chuckled and she chuckled with him.

"I guess they're tired of seeing you mope around."

He drew back. "Mope? I don't mope."

She arched an eyebrow. "And I suppose you've never been grumpy either?"

"I—" He stopped and grinned. "So maybe I can be grumpy once in a while. But you changed all that, Abby." They ducked under a low-lying walnut tree and the foundation for the house he and his brothers had been laying came into view.

"Wow," she breathed. "You've really made progress this week." She let go of his hand to walk closer to the cinder blocks set on the footers.

"No rain and things weren't too busy at the harness shop. Charley Byler came over from Seven Poplars to give us some pointers, him being a master mason." Ethan pointed to her. "I think you met his wife the other day. Miriam?"

"That's right. Miriam Byler." She turned to him, her smile warming his heart. "So show me what's what. Where's the kitchen? You showed me the sketches, but it isn't the same as standing here," she said excitedly. "Show me again. Take me through our rooms."

Ethan clasped her hand again and led her forward. "So here we are on the front porch that will wrap around the house this way and that." He pointed in each direction with his free hand. "And this is the front door and the hallway." He took a big step forward. "Parlor on this side." He indicated the right. "Living room behind it with doors that will open up both rooms when we host church services. And the kitchen is this way." They turned left and walked across grass that had been trampled by many boots that week. "The pantry and mudroom are behind the kitchen. The back door will be in the mudroom, which will also have room for a washing machine and dryer that will run on propane. In the middle of the house, beyond the front hall, will be the staircase and beyond that is a first-floor bath and bedroom. *Dat* and Rosemary's request. At some point, they figure they'll be too old to want to climb steps."

Abigail nodded and kept smiling.

He was so pleased. Because making her happy made him happy. "Upstairs will be another big bathroom and three bedrooms." He took her hand again. "I figured we'd sleep upstairs with Jamie." He moved very close to her and without thinking, kissed her temple. "And with the little ones I hope God will bless us with someday."

She looked at him for a moment, but he couldn't read her face. He was afraid maybe he had crossed the line, kissing her like that, but it had been an act of tenderness more than anything else. As for speaking of children, they'd talked about wanting a family, even about how many children they would like to have.

She took his other hand in hers and faced him. "It's going to be beautiful."

"How can you tell?" he teased, wanting to lighten the mood. "I've not even yet finished the—" Something struck him, stinging his back, and he whipped around trying to figure out where it had come from. It was nearly dark but as the sun had set in the sky, the moon had risen. He could make out the shapes of the trees in the orchard, the pallets of cinder blocks that had yet to be laid and a wheel barrel used for mixing mortar, but he couldn't see—

He was struck again, this time in the chest. "Ouch!" he said, instinctively rubbing where he'd been hit.

"What is it?" Abigail asked. "Did a bee sting you?"

He leaned down and in the semidarkness found a pebble. "Not a bee. Someone just hit me. Look!" He held up the rock.

"Who would hit you?" she asked incredulously. "Maybe we just kicked it up or something?"

Ethan studied the shadows. He was willing to take a guess as to who was pelting him with pebbles, but he didn't have to risk making any false accusations because at that moment he spotted a little boy's face peeking over the wheelbarrow.

"Jamie!" Ethan said.

Abby grabbed his arm. "Jamie wouldn't—"

"Jamie!" he repeated more sharply, calling into the darkness.

Before Abigail could finish her thought, Jamie stood up from behind the wheelbarrow, revealing himself.

Abigail gasped as she saw her son appear. Why would he do such a thing? It had to be a mistake. Maybe he'd been aiming at a predatory animal.

"Come here, please," Ethan said to her son, pointing at the place in front of them.

Jamie slowly came forward, hanging his head. He wasn't wearing his hat.

"Do you understand how dangerous what you did could have been?" Ethan asked, keeping his tone low. "You could have hit your mother. You could have hit me in the eye."

Abigail looked at Ethan and then at her son. "Apologize," she ordered, feeling embarrassed. Ethan sounded awfully harsh, and she still wanted to believe it was all a mistake.

"Sorry. I was just goofing around," the boy said, and she relaxed. He hadn't meant harm.

"It's not playing when it's dangerous, Jamie," Ethan said, looking down at him. "I don't want to see you throwing rocks again unless it's skimming them in a pond. Do you understand me?"

Abigail crossed her arms over her chest. There was no need for Ethan to rub Jamie's nose in his mistake. He'd apologized.

"Do you understand me?" Ethan repeated.

"Ya," Jamie mumbled.

"Goot. Now go back to the house. I would guess your grandparents will be ready to go home soon. We'll be there shortly."

Ethan stood there watching the boy go before turning back to Abby. She could tell from the confused look in his eyes that he was questioning himself, perhaps wondering if he had overstepped his bounds. Yes, he had. They weren't married yet.

When he looked at Abby, she looked away.

He exhaled, and she could hear the frustration in his trembling breath. "Out with it," he said.

She hesitated, gathering her thoughts. Eventually, he'd be a father to Jamie. But he wasn't one yet, and she'd disagreed with his leap to judgment.

"Abby," he said quietly. "Just because we love each other, it doesn't mean we're always going to agree. But when you're upset with me, you have to tell me so and you have to tell me why. You can't think I can read your mind or guess right. And I'll vow to do the same." He opened his arms, looking as disappointed as she felt.

Their romantic walk to see the home he was building for her had turned into what appeared to be a disagreement. "It's the way a marriage should be. Don't you think so?"

"All right." She lowered her arms. "You were quick to snap at Jamie."

"I didn't snap. Actually, I think I was pretty calm considering the fact that he hit me with rocks. Twice."

"More like pebbles," she argued. "And he said he was just playing."

He looked down at her but didn't say anything. Instead, he waited for her to speak again.

She sighed, thinking how foolish it was to defend anyone for throwing something at someone. It didn't matter that it was Jamie. He could have hurt them. "I'm sorry. I'm just not used to hearing someone else correct my son. I know that at school it's your job but…" She let her sentence trail off.

"You think because I'm not his father, I shouldn't speak up when he's done something wrong?"

"*Ne*, you shouldn't," she said quickly. "I'm his mother. I should be the one—" She went quiet for a moment, realizing a time would come when she wouldn't be the only one responsible for Jamie, that people in the community would expect that Ethan, as Jamie's stepfather, would be accountable for his stepson's behavior.

Ethan waited. When she didn't speak, he asked her quietly, "Once we're married, will we share the discipline with Jamie?"

"Of course," she said.

"Okay, so…" He drew out his last word. "Do you want me to keep quiet until after we're married, or do you think it would be better if Jamie begins getting used to it now? You start getting used to it."

She crossed her arms again, ready to argue, then released them as she realized how patient he was being with her, not forcing her to accept this new reality, but leading her gently to it. "You're right," she said in a rush. "I'm sorry, Ethan. You're absolutely right." How blessed she was to have found such an understanding man.

"It's not about being right, Abby. We're talking here about how we want our marriage to be. What you expect of me." He hesitated and then went on. He wasn't acting upset with her. He obviously did believe, as he'd pointed out, that these kinds of conversations were important, even if they weren't easy.

It wouldn't be long before they were married. They needed to settle things like this before the wedding day. Not every issue that could possibly come up could be dealt with now, but when faced with a question, they should at least talk about it. Even if they came to no conclusion yet. Ethan was being wise and prudent, forcing her to confront this important question now: how to handle parenting Jamie.

She took a deep breath and looked up at him. When she spoke, the annoyance was gone from her voice. "I want us to share the parenting. I do want you to give Jamie guidance when he needs it. It's only that... Like you said, I have to get used to it. You know?" She looked up at him. "It's just been me for a long time." And since it had been her alone, she'd often felt the need to be Jamie's defender, to take his side against the world.

"I understand." He took a step closer, smiling down on her. "Think we better get back?" He put his hand out to her.

She took it. *"Ya,"* she agreed. "We best get back before Jamie does something else bad." She shook her head. "I don't know what gets into him. Throwing things at someone? He knows better."

"Sometimes little boys know better and they do things anyway. They can't help themselves," Ethan said as he led her back through the orchard that was now quite dark. "I once threw eggs at my grandmother's friend's buggy. Sadie Basler was her name. Big woman with a *big* voice."

"You didn't!" she exclaimed looking at him, seeing his eyes gleaming in the moonlight. "What would ever possess you to do such thing? Now I'm learning the truth about you, Ethan Miller," she teased, poking him in the chest.

He shrugged. "She tattled on me for snitching snickerdoodle cookies from the pantry before supper. Told my grandmother and got me in trouble. I was about Jamie's age, maybe a little younger. I guess I thought I'd teach Sadie a lesson."

Abby laughed. "By throwing *eggs* at her buggy? And you didn't think you'd get caught?"

"That's where I hadn't quite thought things through. The moment she came out of the house and saw the raw egg running down the sides of her buggy, she knew it was me. I was the only child there visiting my grandparents that day." He was laughing with her now. "Who else could it have been?"

"What happened?" Abby asked. "Did you get a spanking?"

"Worse," he told her, leading her between two blossoming apple trees that smelled fragrant, even in the dark. "I had to clean her buggy head to toe with a scrub brush and buckets of water and then I had to go to her house with her and muck out her goat stalls."

"Oh, no," she laughed.

He shrugged. "I never did it again, so I guess it worked."

"So maybe that's a mistake I've been making." Abby grew more serious. "I talk and talk to Jamie, but maybe there need to be consequences to his actions."

"Maybe," Ethan agreed. Ahead, they could see the lights of his father's farmhouse. It looked like Daniel and June were on the porch saying their goodbyes. "But whatever you want to try, I'll be with you on it."

She stopped and looked up at him. She was still letting him hold her hand. *"Danke,"* she said softly.

"For what?" he asked.

"For being you." Wise, patient, gentle. He would be a good father to Jamie.

And then he smiled at her and her heart swelled with love, as she realized that their wedding day couldn't come soon enough.

Abigail and Phoebe walked side by side down the Millers' driveway. Phoebe was walking her to the road after Abigail had paid her a visit to ask her to stand up with her as her witness at the wedding. Ethan was going to ask Joshua. It had been a tough decision but he had chosen his married brother, thinking it would be wise to have a young couple with some experience, not just beside them the day they were wed, but there to support them in their first weeks and months and years of marriage.

Phoebe had been so thrilled when Abigail had asked her that she had cried. And then she had laughed and hugged Abigail. She had said she would be honored to serve as a witness to the marriage and knew that her husband would feel the same way.

"I wish you could stay awhile longer," Phoebe said as they neared the blacktop road. Halfway down the lane, it had begun to rain, but she had grabbed an umbrella on her way out the door. "It seems like we never have time to visit."

"I know, but I have bread to get into the oven and Jamie isn't feeling well today. When I left, he was playing with his toys on his bed upstairs. But come fall," Abigail said cheerfully, "we'll be living just across the orchard from each other, won't we?" They walked side by side with Phoebe holding the umbrella between them. It was black and plenty big enough to protect them both.

"*Ya*, I suppose that's right," Phoebe agreed. "We'll practically be sisters then."

At the mailbox, the two young women halted. Abigail could hear the sound of hoofbeats, and she spotted a buggy pulled by a bay coming down the road toward them. Because the buggies were all black in Kent County and several families had bay driving horses, she couldn't tell at that distance who it was.

Phoebe backed out from under the umbrella, looking upward. "It's still coming down. Here, take the umbrella." She thrust it toward Abigail.

"I couldn't." Abigail felt silly that she'd left the house without one. The sky had been dark all day. It had only been a matter of time before the rain began. "You'll get wet going back to the house."

"I'm only going as far as the harness shop. Take it." She passed the umbrella to Abigail. "I was going to stop by to find Joshua. He's either there or in the greenhouse."

"You sure?" Abigail asked, holding the umbrella over both of them.

"Positive. I only—"

"Abigail!"

Abagail turned in the direction of the road. Someone was calling her name. A man. Someone in the approaching buggy.

"Abigail!" The driver hung out of the buggy's open door. "Come quick!"

Abigail saw it was Eli as he reined in his horse. "What's the matter?" she called, passing the umbrella back to Phoebe as she hurried toward the buggy.

"You have to get home. Get in. I'll take you."

"But why?" Abigail demanded as she ran for the buggy.

"Your *Dat*'s house," Eli told her, panting. "It's on fire!"

Chapter Twelve

As Eli turned his buggy around in front of the Millers' harness shop, Abigail heard the sounds of the fire engines. By the time Eli turned onto her father's lane, there were already two neon-yellow fire trucks in front of the house and several firemen on the lawn spraying water on the roof of the back porch. Wanting to keep out of the way of the fire trucks, Eli drove his buggy right up over the grass, headed straight for the house. Abigail spotted her mother first, wrapped in a blanket, standing behind a paramedic truck. A young woman in a blue jumpsuit was taking her blood pressure.

Abigail jumped out of the buggy while the wheels were still rolling and raced across the wet lawn. Her mother was there. But where was Jamie? Had he been upstairs on his bed when the fire started? What if... She couldn't bear to think what might have happened. And where was her father?

"I'm sorry, miss!" a fireman called after her. "You can't—"

Abigail paid him no mind. *"Mam!"* she cried, rushing toward her mother. "Are you all right? Where's Jamie? Where's *Dat*?"

June turned to her daughter. Her face was covered in soot as was her dress. She also looked to be soaked, maybe from the rain that was falling lightly, but it seemed like a lot of water.

When Abigail reached her mother, she grasped her thin shoulders. Abigail was shaking from head to foot. "Where's Jamie?" she repeated.

"Bread didn't rise right," her mother answered. "Thought I'd make it into fry bread. Just a little oil is all you need." She smiled at Abigail, obviously having no sense of what was going on around her.

Abigail turned to the paramedic. "I have a son. Nine years old." She could barely catch her breath, she was so frightened. "Do you know where—"

"Found him!" Eli shouted as he led his horse past the fire trucks toward the barn. He pointed in Abigail's direction. "I'll find your *dat*," he hollered. "I'll find Daniel."

"Mam!" Jamie called from behind her.

Abigail swung around to see her son running toward her. Unharmed. Instead of his straw hat, he was wearing a plastic fireman's hat. She opened her arms and hugged him tightly against her. "Where's your *gross-dadi*?" she whispered against him, squeezing him so tightly that the hat fell off.

Jamie squirmed out of her arms and bent down to pick up the hat. "I don't know. Around here somewhere. I just saw him. The firemen had to spray this foam in the kitchen and they were worried the laundry room roof was getting hot so they were shooting water, but *Grossdadi* doesn't want them wetting down anything that didn't have to be wet."

Abigail squeezed her son's cheeks between her hands. "I'm so glad you're all right. How did the fire start?"

She was afraid to ask if he'd done something bad. The other day he'd tried starting a fire in the wood-stove for his grandmother. His heart had been in the right place, but Abigail thought she'd made it plain to him that he wasn't to try to start a fire on his own, not without proper instruction and even then, only when his mother or grandfather was around. "Jamie, what happened?" she repeated.

The barnyard was chaos. Eli's horse had gotten spooked and was dancing sideways as he tried to calm her. There were the two fire engines, the paramedic truck, an ambulance, and now a state police car was coming up the lane. There were chickens running all over the lawn and one of her mother's goats had escaped and was standing on top of the old well house bleating. But none of that mattered. All that mattered was that her family was safe. Abigail took a deep breath and then another.

"It wasn't me this time. I promise," Jamie exclaimed. "It was *Grossmami*," he whispered behind his hand.

Abigail glanced over her shoulder. Her mother was too busy chatting with the paramedic to be paying anyone else any mind. She was explaining how to make blackberry syrup without too many seeds.

Abigail looked down at Jamie. "Tell me what happened, *sohn*."

"I don't know exactly. I was playing upstairs and I fell asleep on my bed and the next thing I knew," he said, placing the plastic fireman hat on his head, "*Grossdadi* was picking me up and running down the steps with me."

"Your grandfather *carried* you?"

"He was so upset, *Mam*. I've never seen him like that. The smoke alarms downstairs were going off and they were so loud."

Hearing that, Abigail said a silent prayer of thanks. When she'd arrived in Delaware, there had been no operational smoke detectors in the house. She'd gone to Walmart and bought several and the batteries to go in them and helped her father mount them on the ceilings and walls, upstairs and down.

"Where was your grandmother when he came upstairs for you?" Abigail asked.

"*Grossdadi* took her outside and then went upstairs for me. We couldn't find her at first. He got so scared that she had gone back in the house. But she hadn't. She was in the henhouse getting eggs. She wanted to make cupcakes, she said," he explained.

"You said she started the fire. Do you know how? Where?"

"In the kitchen. She put too much oil in the frying pan and I guess it dripped? That's what *Grossdadi* said. Then when she lit the gas burner… Whoosh!" He threw his hands up in the air. "I guess when the fire started, she tried to carry the pan out of the house. That's how the laundry room caught on fire."

"Wait." Abigail glanced in the direction of the house. "So the fire was in the laundry room, not the kitchen?" That made more sense now. That's why the firemen were keeping the roof of the porch wet. The porch came off the laundry room.

"I guess," Jamie said. "*Grossdadi* wouldn't let me go inside. I think he put the fire out in the kitchen with the extinguisher we brought from home, but the fire in the laundry room was too big."

"Who called the fire department?"

"Some Englisher who was driving by. She used her cell phone."

Abigail glanced over her shoulder at the house again. She was finally breathing easier. She didn't know how much damage the fire had done, but the house obviously wasn't engulfed. In fact, the firemen had stopped spraying water and were now milling around, talking. She spotted a wagon coming up the driveway at a fast clip and saw that it was Ethan, along with his brother Jacob, as well as Benjamin and Phoebe.

"Can I go see how much of the house *Grossmami* burned down?" Jamie asked his mother.

"You may not." She put her arm around his shoulder and gave him a quick hug. "I'm going to check on *Grossmami* and then *Grossdadi*. You go tell the Millers what happened." She met her son's gaze. "I'm so glad you're all right," she said, emotion choking her.

He made a face and pulled away. "I'm fine."

She watched him run toward the wagon coming up the lane and then she took a breath and walked to where the paramedic was caring for her mother. She saw now that one of her mother's hands was wrapped in white gauze. She couldn't believe her mother had nearly burned down the house. With Jamie in it. Tears filled her eyes.

This changed everything.

That Sunday, Hickory Grove had a visiting preacher because both of theirs were out of town. While Barnabas Gruber led the morning services, Preacher Reuben

Coblenz came from Seven Poplars to preach in the afternoon, following the dinner break. He spoke on the Good Samaritan, a story from the New Testament that apparently, according to Phoebe, he often chose for his message and one that he could speak on at great length. It was one of Abigail's favorite passages, but she had found it hard to concentrate on his message that day. In fact, she'd had a hard time concentrating on much of anything. She'd been avoiding Ethan since the fire earlier in the week and he knew it.

She had chosen a seat near an open window in Eli Kutz's parlor, beside her *mam*. Phoebe was sitting on her other side. Outside the window, a monarch butterfly fluttered. She saw one, then a second and then a third and she realized they were settling in the purple flowering butterfly bush beside the house. She wondered what it was like to be a butterfly. They seemed so free and unencumbered. Like humans, they were one of God's creatures but without the same responsibilities. It was the matter of responsibility that was heavy on her heart today. Had been for days.

Abigail felt someone tug at the sleeve of her black church dress and she glanced at Phoebe.

"You all right?" Phoebe murmured.

Abigail stared straight ahead and nodded.

"Ethan said he tried to talk to you," Phoebe whispered, "during the dinner break, but you told him you were busy."

"I was serving," she whispered back, her gaze shifting to the butterflies again.

She'd not spoken with Ethan since he had come to her at the fire, and even then, she'd been so overcome with worry and fear that she barely remembered what she'd said. He'd offered consolation and help, and she'd thanked him but told him she needed to tend to her parents. He'd understood and told her he'd wait to hear what repairs he could assist with.

Preacher Reuben's voice thundered out, echoing off the rafters as he warmed to his subject and began to repeat himself for the third time. Abigail tore her attention from the window and tried to focus on his words. But as her gaze swept the room, she spotted Ethan sitting across the aisle from her with the other men. As had been the tradition in her church district in Wisconsin, the men sat on one side of the room and the women on the other for services. Ethan wasn't watching Preacher Reuben either. He was staring directly at her. And when their gazes met, Ethan frowned questioningly.

Startled, Abigail averted her eyes, but when she glanced back from under her lashes, Ethan was still watching her. She knew she couldn't keep evading him. That they were going to have to talk, but it was going to be such a hard discussion to have. And she still didn't know what she was going to say. How she was going to say it. When the preacher finally wound up his sermon and the congregation rose to offer the final hymn, she looked at Ethan and found him looking at her again instead of his hymn book.

The hymn ended; everyone sat down, and Bishop Simon offered a traditional prayer in High German before dismissing the congregation to head home to do chores. Because it was Sunday, the only chores that would be done would be those absolutely necessary, mostly involving caring for the children and farm animals.

When everyone scattered, Abigail made a beeline for the kitchen. She'd already told Jamie and her parents she would meet them outside. She just had to pick up the baking dishes she'd brought her rhubarb cobbler in.

There was a crowd of elders at the back of the spacious room, so she turned left to leave by another door, thinking she would go the long way around. When she reached the hallway, however, she found Ethan alone, arms folded, blocking her way.

"What's going on, Abby?" he asked. He met and held her gaze, his face solemn. He was dressed in his Sunday best with black pants, a white shirt and black coat. He wore his wide-brimmed black hat on his head. He was handsome in his church clothes, so handsome that a lump rose in her throat. She had thought she would marry this handsome man. Handsome, good man, but it wasn't to be. Because she didn't have the freedom those butterflies outside the window possessed.

"Why are you avoiding me?" he asked.

"I haven't been avoiding you."

He stared at her, making it clear he didn't believe her. She lowered her gaze. "All right. I have been."

Before she could protest, he grabbed her hand and led her to the rear of the hall where there was an alcove. It appeared to have once been a small room before an addition had been added. Where they stood, no one could see them.

"I thought we were going to be honest with each other, Abby. I thought we agreed that was the kind of marriage we wanted to have."

She clasped her hands in front of her, staring at the floor. She'd chosen her black Sunday dress instead of the dark blue she could have worn because the black was more somber. Because it was a reflection of how she was feeling inside.

"Abby?" he begged. "Please talk to me."

"There you are, *Mam*!"

Abigail turned around to see Jamie coming toward them. He'd grown so much since winter that his black church pants were well above his ankles. The only reason he wasn't flashing bare skin was that he was wearing a pair of his grandfather's black socks that went up higher. "*Grossdadi* says to tell you we're hitched up and ready to go. *Grossmami*'s tired." He made a face. "She says she's tired from wiping down walls at home, but she hasn't cleaned up any of the soot. You and I have been doing it."

"And I'm thankful for your help," she told her son. "You've been so responsible this week. I'm proud of you."

"They can go. I can take you home," Ethan said quietly. "We can take one of the buggies or I can walk you."

Abigail turned back to her son. "I'll be right there."

Jamie hesitated, seeming to sense something was wrong.

"Go on," she told him.

It wasn't until she heard his footsteps in retreat that she turned back to Ethan.

"Abby, what is going on?" he repeated, opening his arms wide. "I know you're upset about the fire, but the house is fine. There are only a few days of work there and the laundry room will be as good as new. Better. And your mother is fine. A few blisters on her hand, that's it." He shook his head. "I don't know how, but it wasn't worse. The Lord keeps an eye on little ones and the elderly, that's what my grandmother used to say. Now I know…"

Abigail barely heard what he was saying. She had to force herself to look up at him. To meet his gaze. Her chest ached. Her heart was breaking. She could almost feel it shattering. She loved him. She loved him more than she ever thought she could love a man again. She loved him and she wanted to marry him and live out the rest of their days together. But life wasn't that simple.

"I can't marry you," Abigail said, interrupting him midsentence.

He stared at her. "What?"

"I changed my mind," she heard herself say. "I can't…I *won't* marry you, Ethan."

He just stood there staring at her for a moment. As if he couldn't comprehend what she was saying. "Abby, we've talked about this. I know Jamie is struggling right now, but he's going to be fine. You heard what Bishop Simon said last time we went to talk with him. That this is typical for a boy his age and to be expected. I think Jamie's already coming around. He came to me during the dinner break and asked me if he could come over this week and help with the framing of the new house."

"It's not Jamie," she whispered.

"Then *what*?" he asked, raising his voice.

His tone made it easier for her to find the words. "I can't leave my mother. She almost burned the house down, Ethan. I have to take care of her."

"You can't live down the road and take care of her?" he asked incredulously.

"Jamie could have *died*," she told him. She shook her head. "I need to stay home and help *Dat* take care of her. You heard the doctor. She said she's only going to get worse. They're my parents. I'm their only child. I have a responsibility to them. Just like as your father's eldest son you have a responsibility to him."

"So that's it?" he demanded. "We're not going to talk about it?"

"There's nothing to talk about," she said, staring at the polished wood floor.

He stood there a moment and then, without another word, brushed past her and walked down the long hall, his footsteps echoing all around her.

Chapter Thirteen

"I figured you'd know what to do," Rosemary said quietly. "I don't know where your *dat* is, but I know your family had beehives back in New York. I know you helped him out."

Ethan's stomach did a flip-flop as he stood at the edge of the orchard and looked up at his little stepbrother Jesse. Rosemary had come to the house site and fetched him just a moment ago.

Jesse, who was almost twelve, had climbed into the branches of a Golden Delicious apple tree and sat with his back against the trunk and his legs swinging down on either side of a branch. He was at least eight feet off the ground, but the distance ordinarily wouldn't have worried Ethan too much. Jesse was strong and agile, and climbed like a squirrel. Like Ethan and his brothers, the boy had been scrambling up ladders and into trees since he'd learned to walk. What scared Ethan at that moment was that Jesse was surrounded by thousands of honeybees.

"Please, Ethan, get them off him and get him down," Rosemary murmured under her breath.

"You stay back," Ethan instructed his stepmother. It was his belief that bees could sense it when people were afraid of them and it made the bees nervous. Nervous bees could be dangerous.

He took a step closer to the apple tree. "Jesse, I need you to sit still and not move," he called to his little brother. "Don't do anything to startle them."

Jesse shrugged. "I don't think they'll hurt me. They like me." Bees surrounded him, walking on his bare feet, his arms and fingers. They buzzed around his head and face and crawled in his hair. And only inches from Jesse's head of brown hair, a wriggling cluster of the winged insects, thicker than the boy's body, swayed on a branch.

"Don't make any noise," Ethan warned, trying to think back to his days of beekeeping with his *dat*. His heart thudded against his ribs.

"They tickle," Jesse said, seeming more fascinated than afraid. He lifted one finger covered in bees and studied them.

"I told you not to move." Mentally, Ethan went through his options. Did he try to brush them off the boy with a broom? Run the hose from the house and spray them with water? But Ethan knew that was foolishness. The bees were already crawling all over Jesse.

Besides, if they startled the swarm, they might all attack both of them. He didn't care about himself, but his brother was still so young. And he was small for his age. The child could be stung hundreds of times in just a minute.

"Please help him," Rosemary said quietly from behind Ethan. "You know how I feel about bees. A snake doesn't bother me. Nor a rat, but bees... When I was a girl, a friend tried to rob honey from a hive. He died. I still remember his swollen body in his coffin."

"No one's going to get hurt here, Rosemary." Ethan took another step closer to the tree, still racking his brain. It was true, they had kept bees back in New York, but that was years ago. He'd never dealt with a swarm himself.

"Could you use smoke?" Rosemary murmured. "I've heard that calms them."

"It probably wouldn't hurt. But I don't think we brought any of our equipment when we moved here. I think *Dat* sold it."

"Where did the bees come from?" she asked.

Ethan glanced up at the swarm. "They've left someone's bee box somewhere, or a hollow tree or maybe an abandoned building."

"Why did they do that?" Jesse asked.

"Probably because their queen was old or the hive got too crowded. They're being so friendly because they don't have honey to protect." He stroked his chin. He'd not grown his beard back. "They're just looking for a new home."

"I see," Rosemary said, staying at a safe distance back, but never taking her eye off her son.

"Were they in the tree when you climbed up there?" Ethan asked Jesse.

Jesse made a face, obviously afraid now that he was in trouble. "I was coming to see you to see how the house was going and I spotted them. I just wanted to see what they were doing."

"Jesse, you're not supposed to mess with bees," his mother called from behind Ethan. "You know better."

"But the bees didn't sting me," Jesse argued as little boys will with their mother. "They like me."

Ethan thought for a moment, then said, "Rosemary, could you do something for me? Could you go to the new house site and get my stepladder? I think it's near the wheelbarrow. Can't miss it." He pointed in the direction of the house he was still working on even though more than a week ago Abigail had told him she wouldn't marry him. Why he was still building it, he didn't know. Maybe because it gave him something to do while he went over and over in his mind how he could change Abby's mind. Which was already proving to be difficult because she wouldn't even speak to him. He'd gone to the house several times to try and even attempted to corner her at Spence's Bazaar, but had been unsuccessful.

"Be right back," Rosemary said, backing away slowly before she cut around a peach tree, moving quickly for a woman in her late forties.

"Honeybees are wonderful creatures," Ethan said, turning back to the apple tree. He kept his tone low and even. "But you have to respect them, Jesse. You have to give them their space."

"So I shouldn't have gotten so close?" His little brother blew a bee off his nose.

"You should not have," Ethan agreed. "Did you know that a community of bees thinks all together, like they have one brain?" he asked him, in an attempt to keep his composure, as well as Jesse's as they waited for Rosemary to return with the ladder. "This swarm has drones and workers, and in the middle, a queen. The others all protect her, because without the queen, there can be no colony."

"Why did they land in this tree in a big ball?"

"They're looking for a new home. For some reason, and we don't know why, they couldn't live in their old house anymore. They won't stay here in the tree. They need to find a safe place where they can store their honey, protect the queen and safely raise baby bees."

"Who taught you about bees?" Jesse asked.

"My *dat*. And his *dat* before him." Ethan heard Rosemary come up behind him and without turning his back on Jesse or the bees, he reached back for the ladder. "I'll take that."

He lifted the ladder onto his shoulder and carried it slowly over to the apple tree. "Hey, Jesse, did you know bees like singing?"

"They do?" he asked.

"Sure do," Ethan said softly. "Why don't you sing to them? Maybe something we sing at church."

In a high, sweet voice, the boy began an old German hymn.

Ethan settled the legs of the ladder into the soft grass and put his foot on the bottom rung and joined his brother in the song. He continued to sing as he slowly, one step at a time, climbed the ladder. When he was almost at the top, he put out his arms. "Swing your leg over the branch," he murmured. "Slowly. Keep singing." His little brother did just as he instructed, and Ethan nodded encouragement. "Easy. That's right. Come to me," Ethan murmured. "Slowly. And keep singing." A bee took flight, leaving the child's arm to join the main swarm. Then several more. Ethan caught Jesse by the waist, and the two of them waited, unmoving, as bees crawled out of his hair and flew into the branches above them. He brushed two more bees off his right arm. "Good. Now we'll start down. Slow and steady."

Sweat beaded beneath Ethan's shirt and trickled down his back. Step by step, the two of them inched down the ladder, and as they withdrew, it seemed that the tone and volume of the colony's buzzing grew softer.

When Jesse's bare feet touched the grass, the last few bees abandoned the child's mop of brown hair and buzzed away. "Go on," Ethan told his brother. "It's safe now. Go to your *mam*."

Jesse ran the fifteen feet or so to his mother and Rosemary gave a little cry of relief as she hugged her son.

Ethan left the ladder where it was and backed up. "We should fetch Eli. He's got bees. He can probably move the whole colony back to his place. They might even be his. Unless you want to keep them," he told his stepmother.

"Eli is welcome to those heathen beasts," she replied.

"Can I go get a snack?" Jesse asked, pulling himself away from his mother, looking embarrassed by her attention.

"*Ya.* But don't eat too much," she called after him as he took off across the grass toward the farmhouse. When he was gone, Rosemary walked toward where Ethan stood, keeping him between her and the bees in the apple tree. "Thank you, Ethan. I'm sorry I pulled you away from your work, but I didn't know what to do."

"It's fine." He took off his hat and fanned himself with it. "I don't know why I'm even bothering with the house at this point. I'll be having no wife to take to a new home."

Rosemary exhaled. "Benjamin told me to hold my tongue and let you and Abigail work this out. But I have to say, Ethan, I think you're being foolish to mope around here when you could be at her house trying to change her mind. That boy will adjust to his mother's marriage. And to you. And you'll adjust to him. He's really not that naughty."

Ethan looked down at his father's wife, contemplating what to say. She was barefoot and wore a midcalf-length dress, an oversize apron with large pockets and a wide-brimmed straw bonnet over her prayer *kapp*. Despite being middle-aged, she was still a pretty woman with brown hair and green eyes. He could see what had attracted his father to her physically, but the person she was inside was even more attractive. Rosemary was smart and fun and she was easy to talk to. She had a way of getting him to tell her what he was thinking when no one else could. Like Abby.

He put his hat back on his head and gazed out through the orchard in the direction of the foundation of a house he feared he would never live in. A house he didn't want to live in without Abby. He hadn't told his father and Rosemary exactly what had happened between him and Abigail. He hadn't told anyone, not even Joshua. He'd just said the wedding was off and refused to say more, even when Joshua had cornered him in the buggy workshop, demanding to know why his brother would let a girl like Abigail get away.

Ethan surprised himself when he looked at Rosemary and said, "We didn't break up over Jamie."

Rosemary appeared startled by the news. "You didn't? I just assumed—we assumed—" She glanced at her fish pond in the backyard that was surrounded by rocks that were covered in moss.

It was twenty by ten feet maybe, oblong, with a bubbling cascade, miniature lily pads, cattails and decorative rock border. The pond, the Irish moss and the wrought iron bench were already there when his father had bought the farm. One of the reasons he said he bought it was because Rosemary had loved that pond with its running water. It reminded her of the streams in upstate New York, he had said.

Rosemary took her time in speaking. "Your father and I just assumed… The way Abigail is with the boy, spoiling him so, him throwing rocks at you here and then after the fire at their house, we thought—" She sighed. "Ethan, we just assumed he had set the fire."

He considered remaining silent, but after spending months talking with Abby, he was finding it harder to hold back his thoughts and feelings. With anyone. It was as if a dam had broken and he was tired of feeling so isolated and alone. "Jamie didn't start the fire."

Rosemary dropped her hands to her hips. "He didn't? Then who—" She halted midsentence, raising one hand to her forehead. "*Ach.* Of course. It was June, wasn't it?"

"You know she saw the doctor. The diagnosis isn't good, Rosemary." Ethan shifted his gaze to the swarm of bees in the tree that was still undulating. He'd quit work for the day and go see Eli. If Eli couldn't come himself, Ethan would borrow the equipment he would need to capture the bees. All he really needed was a nuc box and maybe a little lemongrass oil to lure them in. The bees would find their way into the temporary home within a few days and he'd either give them to Eli…or maybe start his own hive. He had enjoyed working with bees when they'd lived in New York.

"So…this is all because of the fire?" Rosemary asked. "Because Abigail doesn't want to leave her mother?"

"Exactly," Ethan agreed still staring at the swinging, wriggling mass of bees hanging off the apple tree.

"She needs to stay home with her *dat* and help take care of her *mam*."

"Okay…" Rosemary spoke the word as if there was something she didn't understand.

"Okay what?" He opened his arms wide, frustrated more with the situation than Rosemary, but unable to keep it from his tone. "It's over. The betrothal is broken and we won't be marrying."

Rosemary frowned, her hands on her hips again. "Have I missed something here?"

"What do you mean?" he asked impatiently.

"You love her, and she loves you, *ya*?"

He looked away, surprised by the emotion that had suddenly welled in his throat. *"Ya,"* he managed.

"Then why don't you just marry and live there instead of here?"

"Live there?" Ethan wiped his eyes with his hand, embarrassed by the wave of emotion he felt just talking about Abigail. He gave a little laugh that was without humor. "You know I can't do that. I'm the oldest son. *Dat* is depending on me. *Dat* needs me to take care of the farm, to care for the two of you when you get older. He's even got me building the house you'll live in someday so I can take over the big house. I can't live at the Kings' farm. My responsibility is here."

"You have all of these brothers and sisters. I don't think all these chickens are going to fly the coop, Ethan."

"But I'm the oldest son," he repeated. "You and *Dat* are my responsibility."

She narrowed her gaze. "You haven't talked to your father about this, have you?"

"Nothing to talk about," he answered doggedly. "I know my duty."

"Ach." She shook her head, walking away almost as if she were fed up with him. "You Miller men, you're a stubborn bunch. Your mother always used to tell me that. She loved you all dearly, but you sorely tested her patience sometimes."

She turned back and was quiet for a moment, as if trying to decide what to say next. That was fine with Ethan because it gave him a moment to regain his composure.

Rosemary made a clicking sound between her teeth. "I need to get back to the house to check on the little ones. I'll thank you again for getting Jesse out of that nest of bees." She waggled her finger at him. "But I have one thing to tell you, Ethan Miller. You best think on this matter of you and Abigail and talk to your *dat*. Because most people don't get the chance to love again. And you'd be a fool to let her go."

Abigail glanced at her *mam* and then turned her attention back to Rudy, one of their driving horses. She eased him onto the shoulder of the busy road to allow a line of cars to pass. The gelding was a young horse, and Abigail didn't completely trust him yet, so she liked to keep a sharp eye out for traffic.

"We going for groceries?" Her mother's soft voice carried easily over the regular clip-clop of Rudy's hooves on the pavement and the rumble of the buggy wheels. The rain, which had held off all morning, was coming down in a spattering of large drops.

"Ne, to Edna Fisher's for a quilting frolic." She almost added "remember" but caught herself. There was no need to say it. Her mother obviously hadn't remembered where they were going even though they'd left

their house only half an hour ago. An ominous roll of thunder sounded off to the west and Abigail flicked the reins to urge Rudy into a trot as she pulled back onto the road.

"I don't quilt much," her mother announced, folding her hands neatly in her lap. "At least I don't think I do. My sister May, now *she* was a quilter. Log cabin, bear claw, diamond, she could sew all the patterns. Gave your father and me a quilt as a wedding gift, she did. Still have it."

Her mother smiled at her, and Abigail was struck by how pretty she still was even at seventy. This afternoon she was wearing a lavender dress with her black apron, and her black bonnet tied over her starched white *kapp*. "You must have been a beautiful bride, *Mam*."

Her mother giggled. "What a thing to say. I hope I was properly Plain."

Her mother had had a good life, but certainly not an easy one. She had lost more babies than she cared to count, and Abigail had come at a time when her parents had thought there would be no children. But her mother had always been a positive person, kind, faithful and she never resented or bemoaned what she didn't have. She'd always told Abigail and anyone who would listen how God had blessed her and her husband with a child at the age when parents could truly appreciate such a gift.

Unexpected tears suddenly welled in Abigail's eyes and she fixed her gaze on the black pavement spattered with rain ahead of them. What if she was like her mother? What if Jamie was the only child she would ever have? She and Egan had dreamed of a houseful. And then, after she met Ethan, after they had fallen in love, they had talked of filling their home with children, of welcoming, with open arms, as many as God saw fit to give them.

Abigail swallowed hard as she guided the buggy onto Edna and John Fisher's long dirt lane. She hadn't spoken to Ethan in nearly two weeks, not since she had ended their betrothal at Eli's house. He'd come by her father's place three times and then tried to corner her at Spence's Bazaar on Friday, but she'd refused to speak with him. What was the point? She'd made up her mind.

Abigail's father had questioned her about the breakup, but she'd given him no explanation beyond that it had been a mutual decision. As for her mother, no matter how many times Abigail reminded her that there was to be no August wedding, June went right on making plans and talking about the event to anyone who would listen. For that reason, Abigail had been hesitant to bring her mother to the quilting frolic. What would she do if her mother started a conversation about the marriage in the quilting circle? But the creases around her father's mouth and his clipped tone that morning had suggested he needed a break from his wife, so she'd yielded to his suggestion. He had said it would be good for Abigail and her mother to get out of the house, but what he really meant, she suspected, was that it would be good for him to have a few hours' break from June.

When Abigail had agreed to go to the quilting frolic, her father and Jamie had made plans to go fishing on their pond where bass had been stocked by the previous owners of the property. Originally, her father had planned to put another coat of paint on the remodeled laundry and mudroom, but Jamie had cajoled his grandfather into playing hooky for an hour. When Abigail and her mother had gone down the lane in the buggy, she'd spotted her father and son cutting across the meadow toward the pond, fishing rods on their shoulders.

When the buggy neared the two-story farmhouse, Abigail saw several of the Fisher children in the yard taking charge of the guests' horses. As she reined in Rudy, she spotted Phoebe standing near the back door. Waiting for her.

Suddenly, Abigail wished she hadn't come. Not only had she been avoiding Ethan, but she'd been avoiding Phoebe, who was her best friend there in Delaware. The look on Phoebe's face as Abigail took her time getting out of the buggy and then helping her *mam* down was easy to read. Abigail wasn't going to be able to dodge Phoebe this time.

"Sarah!" Phoebe called to one of the teenaged Fisher girls who was hustling across the driveway, carrying a pie brought by the Gruber girls. "Take June inside before she's soaked." Phoebe marched across the driveway, ignoring the rain, and put her arm around Abigail's mother. "Go with Sarah, June. We'll see you inside."

June bobbed her head and went along quite readily. "My daughter's marrying the schoolmaster, you know," she started off, telling the teen.

Abigail groaned and reached into the back of the buggy and pulled out the dish of blackberry buckle she and her *mam* had brought.

"Give me that." Phoebe grabbed the dish out of her hand and passed it to another one of the Fisher girls. Abigail didn't even know which one she was, though she seemed to be close in age to Jamie.

"Now you come with me." Phoebe grabbed Abigail's hand and tugged, making it clear she wasn't going to take no for an answer.

"Where are we going?" Abigail protested.

"Somewhere where we can talk alone." Phoebe impatiently pulled her along beneath the overhang of the barn roof. "Because Joshua and I, all of us, have had about enough of Ethan's moping. And if he won't do anything about it, you're going to have to."

"Ethan's moping?" Abigail asked as Phoebe led her around the corner of the barn, away from the prying eyes of the women arriving for the frolic. She knew he had been upset, but somehow she'd convinced herself that she was suffering more than he was. She could stand her own sorrow, but to think of her beloved in pain...

"Honestly," Phoebe said when they were out of earshot of anyone else. "I don't know what I'm going to do with you. Why did you two break up? What's going on?"

"What does Ethan say?" Abigail murmured, pulling her hand from her friend's.

"No more than you." They stood near a Dutch door. The top was open and the comforting sounds of cows chewing their cud and chickens clucking came from inside. Rain pattered on the tin roof over their heads.

Abigail wrapped her arms around her waist and gazed out into the yard, watching the raindrops fall into a puddle and disperse in circles. "This is between Ethan and me. There's no need for anyone to be involved. We're not teenagers."

"Well, you're acting like teenagers!" Phoebe stared at her for a moment, then exhaled. "Maybe if you could tell me what happened?" She hesitated and then went on. "Eunice is telling everyone that Ethan decided Jamie was too much for him to handle. That that was why he broke up with you. I bet she's told the story about him riding Karl Lapp's cow a dozen times in the last week. I asked Ethan straight out what happened, but he basically told me to mind my own knitting."

Abigail peevishly wiped at a tear that slipped down her cheek. She wasn't ordinarily a crier, but she'd certainly become one since the breakup. "Ethan didn't end our engagement. I did."

The words came hard for Abigail. She didn't understand how once a heart broke, it could keep breaking. But that was how she felt. Every time someone mentioned Ethan's name, every time she saw him, even from her bedroom window when she pretended not to be home, another tiny piece of her heart broke off. She knew she had done the right thing, but that didn't make it any easier.

"Are you mad? Why would you end the betrothal?" Phoebe asked incredulously. "The two of you are perfect together. Even his brothers say so."

Abigail met her friend's gaze. "We should go inside. You don't want to catch a chill." She lowered her gaze to Phoebe's belly that had the slightest roundness to it. She and Joshua were expecting their first child together. It wasn't something talked about openly among the Amish, but Phoebe had shared her secret a few weeks ago and Abigail had been thrilled for her. At the time, she had prayed she would be expecting the following year, but now that hope had gone out the window with so many others.

"We're not talking about me right now. We're talking about you." Sadness crossed Phoebe's face. "Oh, Abigail. I hate to see you like this. So sad. But this is just further proof that you and Ethan belong together. I can't tell which of you is more miserable without the other."

Abigail reached out and grasped her friend's hand. "Can we please not talk about this anymore?" She met her gaze, her eyes filling with tears. "Because I just don't think I can bear it."

Phoebe threw her arms around Abigail and hugged her tightly. "It's going to be all right. I'm praying for you and Ethan. We all are. God will make it right," she whispered in her ear. "He has a solution to our troubles. He always does. Even when we can't see it."

Abigail nodded, taking a shuddering breath. Praying Phoebe was right.

Chapter Fourteen

Ethan heard his father call his name, but he was sorely tempted to pretend he didn't.

He raised his ax and swung downward, relishing the feel of the resistance of the log. He lifted the ax and swung again. His hands were blistered from the rub of the wooden ax handle, his shoulders were aching from the exertion and his eyes stung from the sweat on his face. But none of it compared to the agony in his heart.

He missed Abigail so much… He missed the life they could have had. The life they had dreamed of together. And to think it was all because they both felt so strongly about their responsibility to their families. Once his initial anger had passed, he realized that even if he didn't agree with Abby, he understood her decision. And respected it.

"*Ya*, here," Ethan called. This time, when he struck the log squarely, it split with a satisfyingly loud crack and the smell of fresh-cut applewood filled the air. He had halted work on the *grossdadi* house days ago and started a project he and his brothers had been talking about since they moved to Delaware: cleaning up the old orchard.

"Could you hide a little closer to the house?" his father asked as he came around the wagon, limping slightly. Just after sunrise Ethan had driven the horse and wagon across the pasture and down the old logging road to the orchard on the rear of the property. The trees were all dead, disease ridden or too old to bear fruit and needed to be cut down. It was barely noon and he already had the wagon half-filled with split wood. Ordinarily, he would have loaded larger logs into the wagon and taken them to the woodshed to cut there, but he wasn't in the mood to be near his family. Truthfully, he figured he was doing everyone a favor by staying away and sparing them his "storm cloud," as his stepsister Ginger was calling it.

"I'm not hiding," Ethan grumbled. Setting the ax into another log, he picked up the splits of wood, carried them to the wagon and stacked them neatly.

"Ne?" His father glanced in the direction of their plow horse, Carter, grazing contentedly in the shade of a walnut tree. "Looks like you're hiding."

Ethan wrenched the ax from the applewood stump. "You shouldn't be walking so far. Your hip is just starting to get better." He swung the ax into the wood so hard that the force of the impact reverberated up his arms to his shoulders.

"Enough." His father leaned on the wagon with one arm and raised his other hand. "Put the ax down, *sohn.* We have to talk."

Ethan sank the ax into a stump and rubbed his hands together, easing the soreness of his palms.

"I spoke with Rosemary."

Ethan met his father's gaze. *"About?"*

Benjamin frowned. "You know well what about."

Ethan pulled his hat off, tossed it on the tailgate of the wagon and reached for the jug of water he'd brought with him. He took a couple of swallows and wiped his mouth with the back of his hand. "Rosemary has no right to interfere."

"She has *every* right," Benjamin answered firmly. "As my wife and your stepmother." He waggled his finger at his eldest. "You'll understand one day when you have children. It doesn't matter how old they get, it doesn't even matter once they have children of their own. You're always still a parent and you always want what's best for your child. Even if he's too foolish to realize himself what's best for him," he added.

Ethan eyed his father and then took his time pulling his handkerchief from his pocket and pouring water on it. He wiped his face with the cool, wet cloth. The July heat was oppressive. It had to be well into the nineties.

"Rosemary could tell me that Abigail's mother has been diagnosed with a serious illness. That Abigail made the decision she needed to stay home and take care of her."

Ethan said nothing. He was angry that Rosemary had told his father about their conversation from the other day. But he should have expected that. His father and Rosemary were like that. They never kept anything from each other. And he didn't blame them. It was the way a marriage ought to be.

"We're not like Englishers," his father said. "We don't accept social security or Medicare or any of those trappings. We take care of our own. That said, as an only child, Abigail is right to choose to stay with her parents."

Ethan looked up. For some reason he had expected his father to say he disagreed. To tell Ethan he should go back to Abigail and persuade her to marry and come with him because that was what God intended. For a woman to marry and go with her husband, wherever that might be. Men liked to quote from the Book of Ruth, "Wherever you go, I will go. Wherever you live, I will live." Of course it wasn't referring to a wife, but that was a detail not often picked up on.

"I agree that she needs to be with her parents," Ethan responded quietly. "So that's that. The end of the matter. There will be no wedding." He tossed the wet handkerchief over the side of the rough-hewn wagon's side and walked back toward his dwindling pile of logs.

"What are you talking about? That's not the end of the matter," his father barked, crossing his arms over his chest. "The solution is simple. If Abigail can't come to you, then you go to her." He motioned impatiently in the general direction of Daniel King's farm. "You marry her, and you take on her family as your own. You take her burden on your shoulders, lightening her load."

Ethan stared at his father in disbelief. It seemed as if his whole life his *dat* had been telling him he had a responsibility, as the oldest son, to remain at his side. "But I have to be here for you and Rosemary and Josiah and James."

"Says who?" Benjamin asked.

"You." He pointed at his father. "You made all of these plans for me to stay here and raise a family. Won't you be disappointed in me if I don't remain here to care for you?"

"I don't say this unkindly, but you're not my only child. And Abigail *is* June and Daniel's only one." Benjamin threw his arms around Ethan who was a full head taller than his father. His voice choked with emotion, he said, "I'll only be disappointed in you if you *don't* marry Abigail. If you don't go and care for her family." He drew back, gazing into Ethan's eyes, obviously unashamed of his tears. "I'll be disappointed if you don't take the gift God has given you. The gift we've all been praying for since you lost Mary. And that's a new life. With Abigail."

There was no doubting his father's sincerity. Ethan knew his *dat* wasn't just saying these things to make him feel better. He truly would be disappointed if Ethan didn't act. He believed God had sent him Abigail, and to ignore this gift would be like turning his back on a true Godsend.

With crystal clarity, he realized how right this was, and how it was his responsibility to convince Abigail of its rightness, too. To continue to mope and brood would be selfish.

Ethan took a shuddering breath and hugged his father back. He was nervous, but prepared to act.

An hour later, he was showered, dressed in his Sunday clothes and walking up the Kings' driveway. The old border collie, Boots, greeted him and served as escort, taking him right to the backyard where the family was having dinner at a picnic table beside the house, shaded by a giant silver maple tree.

"Ethan?" Daniel half rose from the bench when he spotted him. "Good to see you. Would you like to join us for dinner? There's still a little something left." He pointed to the remnants of the meal on the center of the table. "We've got cold fried chicken and salads here, and blueberry pie for dessert in the kitchen."

Abby sat quietly beside her son, keeping her eye averted.

"I didn't come for dinner." Ethan removed the black hat he reserved for his Sunday best. And for marriage proposals. His gaze shifted to Abigail. "I came to..." He took a breath. "Abby, I came here to ask for your forgiveness for being so thickheaded. And to ask you to marry me. Again."

Abigail just sat there for a moment stunned. She was so happy to see him, but nothing had changed. Why would he come here and—

"Now, before you say anything, Abby, I want to tell—I want to tell all of you," Ethan said, opening his arms wide, his hat still in his hand. "That I want to come here to live. To help you, Daniel," he said to her father. "To be the best son-in-law and stepfather I can be," he said, addressing first her mother and then Jamie.

Abigail rose from the bench, her heart thudding in her chest. She was afraid she was dreaming but Ethan offered his hand to her and she took it and felt the heat of his touch. This was real. He was there in flesh and blood.

"Would that be agreeable?" Ethan asked her father. "For me to join your family after we're married? To live here and help you take care of the farm?"

"It would be more than agreeable," her father answered. "I'd be proud to have you here. Now come on you two," he said waving at Jamie and his wife. "Let's leave Abigail and Ethan to themselves for a few minutes and we'll see to that blueberry pie."

"Pie!" Abigail's mother declared. "I love a good pie. With a big scoop of ice cream on top."

Jamie giggled. "Me, too, *Grossmami*. Lots of ice cream."

He glanced over his shoulder and it was on the tip of Abigail's tongue to ask him how he felt about the idea of Ethan living there with them. She decided against it, though, and turned back to the man she wanted to spend the rest of her days with. Who she married wasn't up to Jamie.

"Are you certain this is what you want?" Abigail heard herself say. She looked into Ethan's dark eyes, losing sight of her family. The only person that mattered right now was Ethan. "It's a big sacrifice."

"I'm certain I want you," he said, taking her hand. "So not a sacrifice at all. I just—" He exhaled. "I'm sorry I made a mess of things. I'm sorry I wasn't thinking clearly. I wasn't communicating clearly. It didn't occur to me that I could join you here because I thought my *dat* expected me to remain on the farm with him. And care for him and Rosemary in their old age."

"But he's okay with it?" she whispered, looking up at the face she hoped she would be looking into for a very long time. "He's not disappointed?"

"When I finally confessed what had happened, he thought I was a fool." He chuckled. "He said he'd be disappointed in me if I *didn't* marry you and join your family here."

"But you're the oldest son."

Ethan shrugged. "Apparently Rosemary and my father are even less conventional than I thought. Their answer was that they had plenty of other children, so apparently as the firstborn, I'm not all that important to them."

For some reason that struck Abigail as funny and she tipped her head back and laughed. And when she opened her eyes, Ethan was very close to her.

"So, will you?" he asked, taking both of her hands as he faced her.

"Will I what?" Of course she knew what he was asking, but she wanted to hear it again.

He smiled, seeming to understand. "Will you be my wife, Abigail? To have and to hold until death parts us?"

Abigail met his dark-eyed gaze as she leaned closer, looking up at him. "I will marry you, Ethan. Because I love you."

"And because I love you," he whispered.

And then, even though they both knew better, when he lowered his head and brushed his lips to hers, she accepted his kiss. He released her hands and wrapped his arms around her and just as they were about to kiss again, something struck them on the tops of their heads and they were both suddenly soaked with water.

With a squeal of surprise, Abigail stepped back. "Jamie!" she cried. "I thought I told you—" She looked up to see that the culprit was not her son, but her mother!

"Ethan and Babby, sitting in a tree," her mother sang, hanging out the upstairs' window. *"K-I-S-S-I-N-G!"*

"Mam!" Abigail shouted up, wide-eyed.

"I'll get her!" came Jamie's voice. Then he pulled his grandmother out of the open window and slammed it shut.

Abigail lowered her gaze until she was looking at Ethan again. He was soaking wet with water running off the brim of his Sunday hat. She covered her mouth to keep from laughing aloud and Ethan began to laugh with her. Her *kapp* was wet, her hair was wet and so was her blue dress.

"Well," Ethan said, pulling a handkerchief out of his pocket and handing it to her. "If nothing else, being married to you is going to be full of surprises."

"Ya," she agreed, wiping her face.

"And also love," he said.

And then he kissed her cheek gently and Abigail realized that God had given her all she had prayed for, and much, much more.

Epilogue

Two years later

Abigail dipped her brush into the bucket of whitewash and drew it across the clapboard siding. The new school year would begin in less than a week and Ethan was determined to get the entire exterior of the schoolhouse painted before his students arrived.

"Have enough paint?" Ethan asked, coming up behind her. He pressed his hand to her shoulder.

"Plenty," she told him, smiling as she dipped her brush again. "Where's Jamie gotten to?"

"He went back to the wagon to get a roller for me. Joshua is using one on the back wall and he says it's going faster." He gazed down at her. "You really don't need to do this, you know. We have plenty of help. You could go sit under the tree with your mother. She's keeping an eye on Joshua and Phoebe's new baby."

She cut her eyes at him and brushed the paint on the wooden siding. "You want to park me under a tree with elderly ladies and newborns?" she asked.

He gazed down at her swollen abdomen and made

a face, indicating it was not him who was being ridiculous.

Abigail was two weeks short of her due date and was enormous. Twins, according to the midwife. But she felt good. And she wanted to be there with Ethan to help him prepare the schoolhouse for the new year. "Stop fussing over me. I'm fine," she told him shaking the paintbrush at him.

He plucked the paintbrush from her hand, wrapping his other arm around her. "Stop fussing, you say? Isn't that a husband's job to fuss over his wife when she's about to give him not one but two more sons?"

His words made her tear up. She'd been so sensitive these last few weeks that she knew her time was growing near. The fact that Ethan referred to Jamie not as his stepson, but his son, filled her with emotion every time he said it. Because he meant it.

When Abigail married Ethan, she loved him, and he loved her. And he had been serious in his promise to join her family. He was up at dawn with her father, milking cows. He plowed, he mowed, he did whatever work was needed on the farm. He and her father had become good friends and Ethan couldn't have been kinder to her mother, even as time passed and she was less aware of the world around her. But Abigail had expected all of that. What she had *not* expected was the love that she had seen grow between Ethan and Jamie. In the first days of the marriage, things had sometimes been tough between the two of them. But Ethan had continued to tutor Jamie and to act as a substitute for his father, not as his father, and against his will, Jamie had begun to soften toward Ethan.

And now, they were the best of friends. That didn't

mean that issues didn't arise when Ethan had to discuss Jamie's words or actions with him, but there was no resentment like the early days. Jamie now accepted Ethan's guidance the same way he did his mother's or grandfather's. And Jamie was so excited now about the prospect of having little brothers to take care of and to act as a role model for.

"I'm serious," Ethan said, kissing her temple. "You've been on your feet for hours. Why don't you take a break? Go check on your *mam*. On the baby. I'm sure Phoebe would appreciate it. She's on the back wall with a paint roller. I think she paints faster than Joshua."

Abigail laughed. The truth was that she was getting a little tired and her back was beginning to ache. She rubbed it absently. "Think we'll finish today?"

"At this rate, we'll be opening those picnic baskets early," he said leaning down to pour paint into a tray. The painting of the schoolhouse had become a family event with the Millers and Kings joining forces.

"Found it, Ethan!" Jamie called, running across the driveway with the roller in his hand.

"Oh, goodness," Abigail said, watching her son come toward them. "He's sore in need of new pants. Everyone in school will be saying he wears high-waters."

"Told you I thought he'd grown a foot this summer," Ethan said, watching him, too.

At eleven years old, Jamie was already beginning to look more like a man than a boy and Abigail was so thankful for the new babies. Because before she knew it, her eldest son would be a man. A fine man, who read well, thanks to her husband. And was kind and well behaved...at least most of the time.

Jamie halted in front of them, out of breath. "I thought

you were going to use the roller," he said to Ethan. "What are you doing with a paintbrush?"

"Your mother was using it, but now she's not." Ethan took the roller from Jamie and handed him Abigail's brush. "I thought you could help for a while. Your mother needs to rest."

"You trust me to paint the school? Sure," Jamie said excitedly.

"I'm not tired," Abigail said with exasperation. "I don't need to—" She halted midsentence as her husband and son turned their backs to her to begin tackling the task side by side. Maybe she wasn't too tired to paint, but it made her so happy to see them working together that she gave Jamie a kiss on the cheek.

"Ew, *Mam*!" her son groaned, pulling away from her.

But she just laughed and turned to plant a kiss on Ethan's cheek. "Thank you," she whispered, looking up at her handsome husband.

He turned to her, paint roller in his hand. "For what?"

"For loving us," she said and then she turned and walk away, stroking her belly, knowing that as good as life was with Ethan, it was only going to get better.

* * * * *

Dear Reader,

I hope you enjoyed Abigail and Ethan's story. How wonderful that they were able to find love again after such happy first marriages.

I always learn something about myself or the world we live in when I write a book and *A Summer Amish Courtship* was no exception. Ethan and Abigail's story reminded me that God created us all more similar than different. Even though the Amish live differently than many of us, they still face the same challenges, particularly when it comes to family. I think the sense of responsibility to our loved ones runs strong in us. I know it does in me. But while families can certainly stress us out, my family is my greatest treasure.

With Abigail and Ethan on their way to living happily ever after, I've come upon someone else in Hickory Grove longing to find happiness again. Eli Kutz is not only looking for a wife to cherish, but a mother for his four beloved children. If you've read previous books in the Hickory Grove series, you'll recall that Eli hasn't had the best of luck in courting. That's about to change. Eli will fall in love with a young woman you would least expect. Which of Rosemary's daughters do you think it will be?

Peace be with you.
Emma Miller